Afterbirth: a novel

Z M Barrett

This edition was published by
Use Your Delusion Books
On 29th March 2021
Copyright © Z M Barrett 2021

This book is sold subject to the condition that it shall not, by the way of trade or otherwise, be lent, resold, hired out, or otherwise circulated without the author's & publisher's prior consent in any form of binding or cover other than that in which it is published and without a similar condition, including this condition, being imposed on the subsequent purchaser.

Also written by Z M Barrett -
Manic
Evergreen BETA
Thirteen
Manic: Remnant
Clouds of Delusion; A collection of short stories
The Phoenix diaries
The Republic
Aimless Musings; Vol IX

Soicals
@zmbarrett13 - the birdy one
@zmbarrett - the pics one
@zmbarrett13 - the facey one

A book can't read itself,
you have to dig through its contents.

It's the same for a person.
They can't tell you who they are,
you have to find that out for yourself.

1

'Spruyt,' the burly voice called. It shook him out of his mindless slumber, a hangover from the past three days sitting on his shoulders. The wooden chair creaked under his weight, the padding long worn down by generations of arses that had used it. With his head whizzing around on his swan-like neck, he tried to find the source of his summons. A somewhat heavyset woman, in her forties onwards, stood with her arms folded on her chest. Clutching at her massive jugs & a notepad covered in hieroglyphs some would sarcastically call English, Spruyt decided she wasn't waiting for him. The voice was far too husky for her. He decided her hair bun had been tied tight to pull the wrinkles out of her forehead. Which worked; it looked as smooth & shiny as a freshly waxed floor. At this, he abandoned his search for the burly voice and thought back to his school days.

    Simpler times. Way back when, he knew what was what. His place in this world. His function & his worth. His worth to himself as well as others. There was a structure in place for him to follow. A structure, whether inside or outside of school, that he rebelled against. What he wouldn't give for that again, a focus of some sort. He'd been left to his own devices & the future was no longer ahead of him but past him. Sitting on that half-arsed chair, he pondered on things he could not change. In a way, think of it like this; if you or me spilt a drink, we'd make an exasperated grunt. Maybe cruse. Then, we'd head to the kitchen for a cloth or wipe or bleach or such, clean up the mess and pour a new drink. Hell, minutes later we'd be laughing about it. At the silliness of it all. We all spill sometimes, it can't be helped, why get so hung up on it. Spruyt though, he'd spill that drink, stop dead, and then stare at the mess he'd created. Ponder on what caused it, wonder how he'd let it happen, and the mess would stay there & soak into his slippers. Such a waste of energy.

    'Spruyt,' the burly voice repeated. Shiny forehead *was* its source. He had to fight hard with the urge to ask her why her voice was so deep or if she'd kept in contact with Thelma or Lousie after the film had been released. What life was like in the dyke. But he didn't, and I'm glad for it. Be arsed trying to get that exchange down on paper.

Spruyt mumbled a weak apology and allowed himself to be led away from his worn seat. Shuffling along, he wondered if he & shiny head had a fight, who would win. Seeing her massive calves striding in front of him so confidently, he decided she would. Easy. He had a big mouth & a weak swing. The trick with that is to give it your all on the verbal to scare your target away from the physical. Most of the time, shockingly, this worked. Most sensible people, even at their most exacerbated, don't want to fight. No, a few swears, squaring up maybe hoping your few friends would step in, pull you back, etc. Spruyt had learned this early, which meant he pushed people. His nose had been broken too many times. Ribs cracked, eyes split, teeth lose. Still, even lacking the bite, he kept the bark up. It was stupid but this was not a sensible man.

    Like the beaten dog he was, Spruyt followed shiny forehead. He kept his head down, despite the ache it was causing his long neck. Heavy weighted were the shoulders for the past three days. For what? He'd gained nothing in those three days, except more body fat, more memory loss & a lighter bank balance. The smell of a cheap gym's changing room suddenly hit him, he hoped that it was coming from the building around him, not him.

  It was him, obviously.

  Shiny head finally led him to a booth made of a desk, an evaluator & one semi-clear screen to split the large desk from one into two. Spruyt could hear the laughing of two elderly women coming from the otherside of the partition. With that pesky hangover still sitting on his shoulders, he felt that it was directed at him. Scratching his elbow, he swallowed hard the urge to kick the desk and leave. Shiny head left, Spruyt began to question his own existence.

  'Mr..?' This happened a lot. In truth, Spruyt had no idea how his name was pronounced either. His only point-of-reference was how his immediate family said it around him as he grew up. So, in case you are stuck, like our handy evaluator man here, you'll be

Afterbirth

okay saying it as such; 'Spew-it.' The English are so arrogant when it comes to language, anything outside the box and they flounder. Panic in the waters of pronunciation. Spruyt was in no mood to hurry or correct the guy either. Judging by his top-button-done-straight-as-an-arrow-tie-soaked-in-old-spice demeanour, there was about a zero-to-one odds he'd get it right.

'Mr…Mr Sprout?'

'Why not,' he mumbled.

'Excellent, excellent. Please…' He gestured with his arm at the chair in front of his desk. Spruyt looked down and saw there was no padding on this one, only cold hard plastic. Placing himself down, the contact of the chair caused him to shiver. The hangover that was sat on his shoulders had now started to defecate down his back. In his mind, he could feel the waste slowly crawling down his back & pooling in the seat of the chair. Spruyt could only hope all this was in his head, not actually happening. He was too scared to check. Bringing his eyes to the gentleman across from him, he could see the glistening sparkle of sweat on his exposed scalp. His neck hung loose with flesh, saggy but somehow wrinkle-free. Eyes buried so deep in his face they looked like empty drill holes. Spruyt brought each of his hands up to hold the opposite shoulder. It was immature body language from a supposed adult. A diet adult, maybe. Spruyt heard another explosion of horrible hyena laughter from the otherside of the partition. He didn't look at the blurred wall of the next space, but his companion did. Still looking there & smiling, he said,

'So, how are we today Mr Sprout?'

Sniffing up hard through his nose brought a gangle of fluid he didn't expect. It took him a moment to compose himself before answering. Spruyt had been to so many of these sit-downs that he knew he could say anything to this opening query without causing any trouble. They were all the same, asking this question, it was asked for the sake of it. The answer was moot. 'I'm here,' he said finally.

'Excellent, excellent,' bringing his focus back from the partition to the paper in front of him, the evaluator's smile was wiped off. It didn't fade, it was just gone. It's business time.

Afterbirth

'So, you've been on our allowance for…eight months or so?' Spruyt didn't know or care and wanted to say as much, but couldn't. Answers were not only being listened to now but were also being noted for good measure. He answered in the affirmative, through a mumble or nod or both.

'Righto. Now, since your last visit, what have you done to find gainful employment since your last signing-on date?' Again, the answer was a yes and also a lie. Spruyt brought his hands down to his lap so he could watch his fingers dance around themselves. It meant he could look at them instead of those horrible empty drill holes & not think about the flabby fat neck's demanding questions.

'Have we had any progress, then?' Such a preposterous statement, Spruyt thought. First off, progress is a relative term. The past two weeks had seen vast progress in the following; how far he could spit (hitting almost seven feet now), how many times he could wear a pair of socks before they were noticeable & needed washing again (five days), or how many cans it took to fill up the recycling sack (three-hundred & fifty uncrushed, crushed research was to commence within the next two weeks). In Spruyt's eyes, this was progress. Something gained, something learned. But, thinking all that, he also knew this would not be progress for tiny empty eyes, for drill holes here. And secondly, *we*? Come on guy, at what point are ***you*** involved? Spruyt was biting through his tongue at this point trying not to say this, trying not to say anything to empty drill holes, that you are not even involved in these visits. Asking banal questions and then handing me a ticket to move on, an Argos of unwanted labour, useless members of this here great society. Spruyt wanted to say all this, turned all this around in his thoughts, but what he actually said was, 'Promising vibes from some interviews. Nothing confirmed yet though, you understand.' He let out a small, laboured cough.

    Spruyt hadn't been for an interview since he gained his last job several years earlier.

    Cue, 'excellent, excellent...'

The scribble of a pen against cheap paper filled Spruyt's ears until it was broken by the rip of a ticket.

'So, here is your number Mr Sprout. If you'd check the automated job kiosks on your way out if you haven't already, it would be greatly appreciated. You have a great day now.'

He slammed the door shut. It wasn't meant, Spruyt was just heavy-handed at times. Clumsy. The wind had picked up and left him with a chill. Standing behind his closed front door, he held his face in his hands. Already, the smell of stale ale met his nose. Shuffling his feet but reminding in place sent sounds of crackling paper cascading around him. Letters, takeout menus, sales, taxi adverts, all the world's offers had piled up at his feet. Which he ignored, didn't read and trampled all over. He ascended his narrow staircase and climbed into his bed.

This was a three-bedroom house and Spruyt preferred to use the back room. It wasn't the main bedroom or even the largest, but it had been his before the rest of the house was. Also, it was close to the bathroom which was often needed. Fully clothed, he climbed into bed. It was early afternoon but the outside window had a grey sky that could have been early morning or early evening. Spruyt pulled up the dirty covers and thought about taking his shoes off. He decided against it as it seemed like too much effort. He rolled over onto his side and slept uneasily.

Spruyt's house wasn't located in the best part of town. No, but it was all he knew. All he had. It was left to him by his Nan, paid for and homely. He started off in it with the right intentions. Engaged, working the nine to five, saving for a wedding, painting at the weekends, jogging in the evenings, making homemade guac, attending protests for his liberal left-leaning stance on most things. All that was in the past now. No interests, no hobbies. Deep down, he knew he'd tried and failed, and that was that. No trying again, not on your life. Me or you, we hit hurdles, crash to the floor, get up and go again. Tears in our eyes and pain in our chest, we move forward. Not Spruyt; he'd fallen and gone fetal. His tear ducts had run dry, his limb's wasted away so even if he wanted to, he couldn't get up.

Which is where we find him now.

The house itself was large even for two/three people. Built before modern regulations ruined everything, the rooms were more wide than tall which left you with a funny feeling. They looked big but due to the low hanging ceilings you still felt boxed in. The kitchen & bathroom had been replaced initially but the rest of the house was still a "work-in-progress," before it was eventually abandoned. Now, all those fancy modern taps and sinks are crusted with mildew, black mould and years of cooking stains. An end-terrace meant he only had one neighbour the otherside of him to worry about who had passed away years ago. The house had remained vacant since. The houses directly across from him were vacant too. Spruyt often thought it was him, he was the issue. Like a bomb, they'd cleared a radius around his house to keep everyone safe in case he went off. He could never decide if this was freeing/empowering or cripplingly sad.

™© *Z M Barrett*

Spruyt woke-up sometime before midnight. He took a trip to the can, emptied his bowels and bladder, washed his face. He went downstairs to see what was in the fridge; he was greeted with a lime with a month old fuzz beard and two jars of mayonnaise. Why do I have two, he thought. Then he pondered too on why he had glass jars instead of the more modern squeeze-easy bottles mayo normally came in. Another modern mystery. He climbed back up the narrow stairs and got back into bed. This time, he removed his shoes along with his jacket and socks. Almost like a grown-up.

    He slept some more.

The second time around he didn't recall ever waking, he just found himself staring out the window. There were no curtains to close. It was still grey outside like the slumber of the past several hours hadn't even taken place. The bland greyness of the sky bore into his head. Spruyt sat up then swung his legs over the side of his bed. Tears dripped down his eyes with no emotion. Subconscious feelings, he thought. Or maybe he wasn't closing his eyes properly as he slept. He left them there for several moments before wiping them away with the back of his hand.

Back to the bathroom he went, but this time he stripped and had a shower to wash away the days from before. Shaving with a month old razor waged war on his long neck and pebble-dashed cheeks, leaving them cut and bleeding. Patching himself up, he walked downstairs to assess his empire. That smell, he thought, is getting worse. It was like a zoo crossed with a skip set on fire crossed with an open sewer nearby. All that and more. He looked in the kitchen drawer, fishing out a pair of workman gloves he had no idea he owned. Bin-bags were the end game here, but it soon became clear he didn't have any. Sighing heavily, he put both hands on top of the grubby modern kitchen counter. He held this position for several moments, head down, each arm far apart like the leg-ends of a cheap set of swings. His arms were just as thin as those poles to be fair, his chest and legs too. He sighed again.

Off to the shop for supplies, he accepted.

™© *Z M Barrett*

Spruyt was waiting at a traffic light. The traffic was non-existent but he didn't trust himself to cross the road on his own judgement. A grown man, unable to trust himself to get safely across the road. How the mighty have fallen, he pondered.

Looking up, Spruyt saw the solid green light of permission. The breeze picked up a little causing him to shiver. Eventually, the light jumped up to amber. Just as it flashed on, Spruyt noticed that somebody had drawn a smiley face onto the amber light. It was poorly drawn, wonky in black marker. The once thick line and two dotted eyes had faded over time and attacks from the weather. The eyes had run like wet mascara, ink lines hung from the mocking smile like hunger dribbles and spittal. As the light jumped up again to red, Spruyt swore he could hear that face laughing at him over the wind.

To be able to sell vodka in the United States, legally, it must be a neutral spirit, clear, colourless, odourless, and devoid of character. This is how Spruyt had been feeling for many

Afterbirth

months. A neutral spirit. Clear, colourless, devoid of character, but powerful enough to make you sick if you kept indulging it. I mean, look at everything I have caused in my life, he thought. Look at Marie.

I'm the human form of vodka, Spruyt had often pondered. Normally when drunk.

Bag...he'd forgotten a carrier bag. A bag for life was a big commitment, for sure, but Spruyt had taken the plunge a few times. Still, this left him spending needless pennies on another thing he'd just abandon to one of the modern kitchen cupboards. Hoarding more trash he doesn't need. The whole point of this exercise was to clean up mess, not create more.

Cue the internal battle of Spruyt. His legs went onto autopilot, carrying him forward along a route he'd travelled many times, as his brain tried to convince him to abandon his quest. What was the point, a dark voice said, you are the only one that sees that mess. Your filth is the most interesting thing about you right now, so why destroy it? We'll all die someday anyway, why bother making sure your skirting boards are dust-free? Dull & dark this voice continued on.

It's safe to say when cleaning was involved, Spruyt's nihilistic tendencies really came out in force. He felt that the dark voice was making some valid points. Still, he's legs moved him on. Forward down the path and under the grey sky he went.

The door to the mini-market slid open. One side of it was covered in either a split milkshake or dry sick. A jolt of paranoia shot through Spruyt as he tried to remember if that was him or not. He walked past the baskets without picking one up. In the home section, he found his bin liners. Two rolls he picked up for good measure. Spruyt then decided to get some food for the fridge and cupboards. Darting back through the isles he'd already passed, he picked up packets of things, crisps, biscuits, noodles and the like. Soon, his arms were full and he was cursing himself for not picking up a basket on his way in.

After collecting a mismatch of freezer goods & cupboard stuffers, he saw the till at the other end of the mini-market. A shop worker was sitting there, waiting for

Afterbirth

something to do. Someone to serve. She was all earring hoops and volumized hair. Spruyt wondered how much of the ozone she destroyed weekly just getting ready to come into work.

It was the only till he could see from the aisle he was standing in. Situation critical; his arms were bursting at the seams. He knew from coming in that most of the tills were unstaffed apart from that one. It seemed like fate. Slowly, he waddled down the final isle. Each step took him closer to victory. He was so close, so very very close, when his left arm gave way and dropped all its contents onto the floor. The store was quiet, not many people in, so the crashing sound seemed to fill the entire place. Hoops looked up from her nails, let out a small laugh, then went back to inspecting them. Spruyt dropped his head and sighed. Lifting it up, he saw another offer. He then focused hard on a decision he'd already made. Eventually, he pulled two crates of stuff off the shelf before crouching down to collect his other fallen items.

It was two-for-one on some low dated beer. Alcohol, Spruyt thought, is a lazy man's addiction. Other drugs involve suss characters, tense exchanges, government interference, occasional prison time. Ale, it was much safer when you thought about it. No risk, really, apart from lack of dignity & money.

Despite adding more weight to his arms, Spruyt puts the crates side by side, giving himself a surface to stack the rest of his wanted items on. That dark voice assured him it was fine to get the booze for this reason alone. It felt necessary, like fickle fate always does.

That's what debauchery offered, you see. A momentary bliss. That was the appeal. There were no ties, no pressure, no responsibility, just a vacation from yourself. Or as Camus called it, 'immortality.' Spruyt hadn't realised this yet, but that was what he'd let his life slide into. A messy circle of trying to maintain that immortality.

Throw this in with the fact he also had an overwhelming feeling that he had a task to complete, but not knowing *what* that task was, well, this confusion sustained this

Afterbirth

prolonged mess. Not having the tools to work out what this task was either, meant Spruyt willingly chose this horrible oblong circle of momentary immortality.

That hangover, that comedown though, that was mortality returning. That bitter dry taste on your tongue, that pulsing headache, that ache in your guts, that was your nature returning to its natural place. You can't outrun your being, your nature. Spruyt needed to learn this.

A day later, Spruyt was finally cleaning. He was so exhausted from his trip to the mini-market that when he arrived back home he dropped down on his flat sofa with his new bags. He sat there for several moments before he opened the first crate. The beer smelt like cheap washing up liquid.

Tasted fine though.

After three bottles, he felt mobile again. He got up, put away the rest of the shopping and decided to see if his old record player was working. It was not. Instead, he brought the radio in from the kitchen, placed it on the vacant TV stand and plugged it in. On inserting the plug into the socket, electricity spat out at him like minute lightning. He jumped back, swore at himself and switched the radio on. Music or talking, it didn't matter. He just needed noise. Atmos and a feeling of life. Or the sense of life being lived outside him, and with radio DJ's talking about banal stuff as what they had for tea last night or their current preference in soft drinks, it worked. Spruyt returned to the sofa and carried on working his solo-way through the crates.

When he was halfway through the second crate, guilt crept into him. To try and placate it, he cleared away all the rubbish left from his first crate and his empties filled with sticky smelling backwash. There, half the job is already done, Spruyt thought. He sat back down, checked on how many bottles he had left (three, not including the one he was halfway through), and let out a small, laboured cough. With the radio playing some sort of new-age jazz, he lent back and closed his eyes. The darkness swilled around his eyelids like water. Like a current that has no

Afterbirth

source nor shore. No end, no beginning, just being.

Living in a void all the time isn't easy, but it has its nice periods, Spruyt thought.

When he was down to his last bottle, Spruyt retired up the narrow staircase to Bedfordshire. Stripping down to his boxers, he stood for a moment in the heavy dark. Only a few strands of moonlight broke the otherwise black veil of the night around him. In these few glimmers, he looked down at the derelict mess that was his body. Good job there isn't a mirror in here, Spruyt thought.

He climbed into his bed. Propped up by the headboard & wall behind his bed, he sat in silence and worked his way slowly through his last bottle. Thoughts trotted in and out of his head but he paid no mind to them.

Placing the bottle on the floor, Spruyt accidentally knocked it over. In a puddle of moonlight, he watched the dregs of the bottle soak deep into the carpet. It crawled over the material like a shadow. Lying on his side, Spruyt watched all this unfold. He knew he should feel something about this, but for the life of him, he couldn't work out what it should be. Eventually, he closed eyes but that was only because his open eyes started to feel like grains of sand. He heard the dry skin of his eyelids shift and crack as he closed them.

He wasn't hungover; it was a low percentage and he'd had plenty of training with the ale in recent months. Spruyt could still feel the hangover lurking over his shoulder instead of being on them, breathing on his neck, confused that it should be here but not able to slow him down or interfere with him. All it could do is witness Spruyt's appalling cleaning skills.

After clearing each room of rubbish, he opened a window to try and air out that stagnated aura. Wearing the work gloves he'd found, again he pondered on where they had come from. After some time, he decided it didn't matter, it was just good that they had turned up.

A bang at the door. Spruyt kept his work gloves on as he answered it. 'Mr…Mr…?'

'Yes,' Spruyt said, 'I live here.'

'Superb. Sir, may I ask who you are considering to vote for in the local council elections on the 5th? Because I represent-'

Spruyt slammed the door and went back to his cleaning.

Several hours and seven (yes, SEVEN) bin liners later, Spruyt licked his bowl clean of instant noodles and returned to his bed. It was early evening. All the junk mail had been thrown out, all the empties cleared, and all the surfaces wiped down. He only had a few dish rags, water and some diluted-elbow grease, but it was better than what it was before. The cooker and kitchen tops needed something more potent to be properly cleaned. This would require another trip to the shop, which given his weakness on the last trip, he wasn't brave enough to go back to. Not yet, anyway. Another jolt of guilt came back to him as he thought about the few nights previous, sleeping fully clothed. These were not the actions of a grown man and Spruyt knew this. Still, he couldn't help himself. He rolled onto his side and waited for

™© *Z M Barrett*

sleep to come. It came quickly but was fitful, uneasy.

A phone ringing. It jolted him awake. It had been so long since he'd heard it ring. Panic-stricken, he started looking under his dirty clothes in the room that were within reaching distance of his bed. No dice. He checked under his pillows and duvet, nothing. The ringtone was some dire straits number which only added to his anger. He cursed himself for making such a choice. Spruyt was about to disembark from his bed to look inside his wardrobe but the ringing stopped. He sat upright for several moments, blinking heavily, before sinking back down into his bed. Again, sleep came quickly but was uneasy.

Spruyt got up. On his way out of his room, he recalled his phone ringing. Standing in the doorway with his back to the room, he pondered. He no longer had a landline, who does, so he couldn't ring his mobile. His emotional strength wasn't strong enough to turn around and look through the room again. He'd cleared his house of the rubbish and

Afterbirth

stale bottles/containers, but the rubbish of his past and present life was still to be sorted. Eventually, he decided, if it was important they'd call again. He moved out of the doorway and down the narrow stairs.

The front room was freezing. After eating a breakfast of cereal bars and coffee, he'd decided to dig out an old magazine to read from the front room. Back in the day, Spruyt was big into his craft beer. Not like currently, no. This interest was more academic to the brewing side of ale rather than consuming. He'd known about it in-depth in his former existence; mashing of the dry malted barley, lautering to dry all excess liquid, then the boiling to fermenting to conditioning to bottling. Just like a music or film or writing or art critic, he knew so much of the process behind the product but was never brave enough to try it himself. To create something instead of commenting.

    So, by this standard, he was currently a god-damn artist.

    Walking into the front room left Spruyt feeling like a bucket of cold water had been dropped on him. Searching around, he realised he'd left one of the windows open. Shivering still, he walked across the room and closed it.

Sitting on the stone-cold flat sofa, he no longer felt like reading. His breakfast swirled around his stomach like clothes in a washing machine. He thought about a walk but decided against it due to the cold in the room he was in. He would only be just-as or even colder outside. He looked on to the empty space left by the old TV. The radio was still there and he briefly thought about switching it on before deciding not to. In his mind's-eye, Spruyt saw himself smashing in the screen again. Wrench in hand, wearing an undersized pink tutu and work boots, his past-self was there again destroying the TV, amongst other things.

On remembering, he was both fascinated and shocked by what he did/saw. The memories wanted to flow back to the other things that gave this shocking scene its context but he wouldn't let them in. He needed to slam the door shut on all that. Not today, he thought. Not today. He got up off the cold flat sofa and left the room.

On making more coffee, Spruyt heard his phone ring again. Slamming his mug down, he ran out of the kitchen and up the narrow stairs. Taking two steps at a time, like a person with purpose, he reached his bedroom doorway whilst it was still ringing. That was the easy part, he pondered. I still had to find the prick.

He found himself looking through the areas he'd already checked last time it rang. Frustration grew along with a film of sweat like shrink wrap on his skin. Eventually, he found it stuck between the back of his mattress and headboard. Almost slicing his finger open on the smashed screen, he swiped it open.

He answered, 'Uncle Joe's steakhouse; you kill'em, we grill'em.'

'Paulie! You bastard. It's Gerry; now listen, they've had me locked away again. My god, can you believe it? Putin is up to his old tricks again. Now listen, I questioned that

™© *Z M Barrett*

whole virus thing. It was created, I'm telling you. Listen to me, Paulie! Don't abandon me like the others. Now, think back; why did some countries have a low-to-no infection rate where others didn't? Because the virus was meant for where it landed! Us, the States, China, the rest of the world wants rid of us all Paulie! My wealth of medical knowledge could expose this, Paulie, that's why they have all locked me up again. Now listen…'

    Spruyt let out a small, laboured cough. Gerry was a good man. *Is* a good man. He just can't help himself, the poor guy. He never drank, he didn't do drugs or go to loud rock concerts. He never pigged out on snacks or let his body turn soft and fat through laziness. The man was brilliant in his day. Well respected in his field of medical science. Mainly focused on forensic pathology, from what Spruyt could remember. Histopathology, cell blocks, the history behind the cell change in decay, that sort of stuff. So much time spent reading, researching, learning, years of residency around the country, and for what?

    He's been sectioned again. Spruyt could tell. He knew he should hang up but it seemed unnecessarily cruel to do so. Gerry's words weren't slurred, there were no gaps or pauses, it all flowed naturally from him. It was the content that was a mess. All conspiracy theories laced together with paranoia and anger. The toll this took on his immediate family was nuclear. Spruyt, he was the cousin removed god knows how many times, so he was outside the circle looking in. The worst thing about Gerry was the trigger; no one could work out what it was. The way his wife told it, he came home from work one day all withdrawn and morose. Sullen. He'd been prone to bouts of melancholiness, Spruyt had heard, but we all are. Anyway, he didn't speak at all this one night. He went to bed straight after their evening meal. The family followed suit at much later/normal time that night. They all awoke the next morning to find him standing in the kitchen with noise-cancelling headphones on yelling incoherently into an open microwave, wearing only socks and a white string vest. Nothing left to the imagination, as the rest of the family was told after Gerry's first sectioning.

™© *Z M Barrett*

Spruyt should hang up. He knew, as all of them did, that you can't humour people like Gerry when they are like this. As cruel as it was to just cut them off, letting them wind themselves up more is worse. He just wanted some connection with somebody, anybody. As did Spruyt.

'...meaning that, with the increase in population it takes more food, more space, more resources to keep all us warm, fed, comfortable. It's a cull, damnit! Exactly like those Tory bastards to agree to all this. To have the poor cut down to nothing. Personally, I'd sink my teeth into both Johnson's and Reese-Mogg's throats and rip out their respective wipe pipes. Have you ever seen a trachea exposed, Paulie? It looks like a fleshly hosepipe, they move like panicked snakes too when you try to hold and pull them out. Now listen,'

Spruyt hung up.

He went to a pub. One close to his house, as was his chosen tac. Mostly within walking distance to his front door, no more than 10 minutes on foot from the pumps to his bed.

This limited his options somewhat. That said, Spruyt needed limiting when ale was involved. Venturing further out for him was dangerous. Not only in the bank balance damage on the extra travel costs and drinking more, but he was more likely to get himself in trouble out in the thick of it in town. Due to his previously discussed nature.

      Spruyt didn't have a local, as such, he just hopped from one place to another. He always tried to space out trips to the same place by a few weeks. Why he did this, he was never so sure. That's what he told himself, anyway. He didn't want to be the local drunk, basically. The class clown, the village idiot. It didn't work though, locals and staff would recognise him most of the time. A funny drunk with the occasional disagreement or fight. A good old sort though, that Spruyt. If he'd known they all thought this, he would have packed-in going to any of them. He didn't want to be their drunk, that's what he was avoiding, whether he admitted it to himself or not. But he was.

      Spruyt was low. Hearing Gerry on the phone like that was selfish. Letting him drone on. It'd been so long though since Spruyt had engaged with anyone. Even on a surface level. Hearing a voice he knew, even though it was unwell and spewing absolute tripe, was nice. But he'd wronged Gerry, letting him drone on like that. Guilt for that and a longing for connection brought him out to the pumps.

'Another chief?'

'Fire away.'

He reached into his wallet, checked for notes. He hated these plastic ones we now have. We couldn't even be trusted with paper money now, he thought. What a joke. Spruyt had two or three worths of drinks left in that plastic money, god willing. Sitting at the bar was dangerous. There was no effort needed. It was like being hooked up to a feeding tube in the hospital; the stuff was just pumped into as you sat there comatose.

'Paulie?'

He turned and saw her; he couldn't recall her name. It was one of Marie's friends. Well, an acquaintance was probably more accurate. Normally Spruyt would panic, blurt out something daft like ahoy there or what's cracking darlin' or something as equally as

Afterbirth

moronic. Two ales deep, his aloofness came up, front and centre.

'Hi,' he said.

What a blinkin' playa.

'Oh my god! How are you doing?' He could see it in her eyes. That pained look of sympathy, of pity. He hated that. He wanted rage, disgust, repulsion, vexation, anything but pity.

'I'm drinking on a weeknight, so make of that what you will.'

'It's a Saturday.'

'Is it?'

There it is, he thought. Confusion. Awkwardness. Not much better than pity but it was a start. She laughed a little, more out of the tension than the intended humour, but it broke the uneasiness somewhat, which helped. Somehow the conversation kept going. Spruyt couldn't believe it when she sat down next to him. She had nice legs, was well-dressed and spoke with effortless grace. She wore her dark brown hair tied into a tight bun which sat in the centre of her head. It shined like it had been slicked brill-cream style. Her dark green eyes were warm and inviting. Her nose was on the large side but it fitted well with her small ears and full mouth. Spruyt was having bad thoughts about the girl with no name. Images included.

'Oh hi.'
Spruyt was now facing ahead. He heard another woman's voice talking with his new, nameless friend. They were strained whispers, forceful yet subdued. Spruyt pondered on why people bothered to have arguments in whispers. If they'd just shout at each other he'd not have noticed. But these harsh and restrained voices demonstrated more than words ever could. He was the source of their disagreement, he knew this. He enjoyed this power, as pointless as it was. He heard the other woman walk away, clip-clopping like a newly shoed horsey. Facing front still, he asked 'Is everything okay?'

'Oh, fine. My err… my friends are leaving now.'

'Ahh,' he replied. Spruyt let this sit for a minute before he added anything more to it. His nameless friend was staring hard at the low contents of her drink. 'I'm not an invalid dear, you are bound by no laws, unspoken or common, to stay.'

She laughed. This time it was more out of humour than pity. Those big eyes told him everything. Interesting, he thought.

A large group of people were by the door, getting ready to leave. From deep in the middle of that huddle, a shout sounded off like a gunshot, 'Bye Beth!'

Spruyt's-not-so-nameless friend turned to the group and waved. Now I have a name, he thought. That guilt can do one. He felt better instantly. Now or never, he thought. He knew he didn't have the money to back up his next move, but the four ales inside his system told him he didn't care.

'Drink?'

'I shouldn't...'

'Come on, it's the weekend.' He looked and made note of her last drink. Judging by the type of glass he could see, she was on the martinis.

'Oh, so you know what day it is now?'

'What I can say, I'm a quick learner.'

She laughed again and nodded.

It was now.

It was rare for Spruyt to build a rapport with someone new. At times, talking to him could be exasperating. It was all outrageous claims and deflected jokes. Nothing was ever serious. Which is fine, in the pub, at the match, at family gatherings, house parties and the such. Not so much when things get serious. It just poured fuel on an already raging fire. The last thing you want to hear is a joke or some stupid comment when you want to talk about your future together or about your aunt dying or when you've been made redundant. In his current environment, Spruyt knew he could lay it on thick. Beth did what all good women do in this situation and kept the conversation going. Spruyt could feed off this so they were well matched. Pinging the conversation ball to each other like two skilled table tennis players. As the night wore on, the rallies in words got faster.

>'You have the mad surname, don't you?'
>'No.'
>'Yeah you do, how do you say it again?'
>'Smith.'

'What? You're lying.'
'I am not.'
'Spell it.'
'S p r u y t.'
(Cue a coy smile from Beth.)
'It's pronounced Smith, I'm telling you.'
'So, you're Paul Smith, like the clothing brand?'
'Like the clothing brand? I **am** the clothing brand.'
'Stop it.'
'No, it's true. I've made 3.4 million in net sales while we're been sitting here. Dollar dollar bills ya'll.'
'Then why am I buying your drinks for you then?'
'Just because I'm rich doesn't mean I spend my own money. Use your head. You get rich from **not** spending money. Economics 101, Elizabeth.'

'You can really put them away.'
'Practice and discipline.'
'And loneliness?'
'Ouch.'
(Silence.)

™© *Z M Barrett*

'Do you do any other drugs, apart from the drink?'

'Of course, ale is just the warm-up act. The opener.'

'What's your main vice then, Paul Smith?'

'Fear. I huff it like petrol and get high off the fumes.'

'Does that work?'

'If you have enough of it, sure. An intense but fleeting high, like sherbet.'

'Sherbet gets you high?'

'Oh girl, you're never lived.'

'So, how come you're out tonight then, Beth?'

'Oh, you know. Getting some cheap drinks in before town. Genetic British night out of binge drinking and solid fat takeaways. Nothing special, really. What about you?'

'Research.'

'For what?'

'To see the female species out in the wild, how they react, how peaceful they are, how they interact with others, how their tribes work and so forth.'

'Interesting. And what have you found so far?'

'So far? Inconclusive, apart from the fear, you understand.'

'When did that start?'

'When you sat down next to me.'

'Of course. Makes sense when you think about it, really.'

'Oh really? Pray tell.'

'Well, you're not around women much at the moment, are you?'

'Wow, that's a burn and a *big* assumption. But also true. What's my tell?'

'You looked dressed for a night out at a primary school disco circa 1996.'

'Listen, when your face is this beautiful, the clobber doesn't matter.'

'Really? I thought you own a clothing brand?'

'Ahh, that's different.'

'How?!'

'Other people don't have my face, do they? They need the help. The better threads they have, the more pro-clobber they buy, the better they feel ergo the more the clothes matter. In a way, I'm a humanitarian.'

'So selfless, Paulie.'
'I know, right?'
(Cue a coy smile from Beth while Spruyt played with his short ball glass.)

'So, you gonna huff that fear later?'
'Most likely. You can join me if you want to, but we'll have to find something you are scared of. It'll have to be a big fear too.'
'Well, your surname scares me. **Big** time. As of this moment, I can spell it but not say it. How often can you say that about an English word?'
'Well played lady.'
And so on.

Still, Beth seemed to be enjoying herself, despite Spruyt constantly seeking her validation via laughs or smiles. He too was enjoying himself. There was a creeping fear though, something he couldn't quite put his finger on. Something he couldn't name was swimming in his nerves. He fought it back, stamped it into submission and stayed with Beth. Whatever it was, Spruyt thought, it'll pass.

The longer the night went on, the worse Spruyt felt. Inside, his confidence continued to dwindle. Four ales before, he was flying high. Sinking all his putts and hitting all his pitches out of the park. Another two after this though, he was fluffing his lines and missing his kicks. It dawned on him that Beth knew Marie. Not intimately, from a distance they spoke, but still. This meant she might know things, things that would be hard to erase. As she talked away, Spruyt listened, but part of him was away plotting. How much does she know? He couldn't help himself. A great night was suddenly turning sour. There was a wrench in the machine, hair in the soup, glass in the salad.

    He ordered two more drinks. Beth dropped her chin down to her neck, smiling at the floor. She brought up her right hand to brush back hair that was not there behind her ear. Spruyt saw it. This was his next in. It worked, his timing was back. The hum of the pub grew louder around them. It wasn't busy with people, only with conversations and sounds. Whatever Spruyt said, it started landing again. Even over the barrage of noise, you could hear Beth laughing into her martini.

It's fair to say Spruyt wasn't the only one working through issues. Who could say why Beth was out that night or why she had abandoned her friends for this bloke. Still, they'd connected. They'd enjoyed each other's company, laughed and got drunk. Whatever happened after this, at least they had that. They'd gained something from each other in their own searches for answers and well being.

He opened the door and let Beth in. Spruyt couldn't believe it when the call for last orders was made. The lights went up, going brighter and brighter until there was nothing but white. He offered to call her a taxi so she could go into town to meet up with her friends or head home. 'Well, I'd rather keep hanging out, if that's okay with you?' Stupefied, Spruyt blurted out his house was only down the street. She laughed, then said okay.

Afterbirth

There was no ale in the house, Spruyt knew, so he suggested they stop off at the corner shop on their way over. They walked in silence, only sharing the occasional word about the area or how cold it was. Beth was nervous, she wanted to live a little but to do so involved risks, and this guy was one. Spruyt was conflicted, feeling so happy that he wasn't spending the evening alone for once but still fighting that ill-at-ease feeling of what she knew of his recent past. It was what connected them initially so it must have come up in Beth's mind, at some point at least.

She had, of course, pondered on Spruyt and his recent past. On one of his many trips to the john, she thought about texting Marie and saying she was with him. Things like this can come back on you if you keep them quiet. There was nothing to hide as nothing had happened, maybe nothing would happen. She pulled her phone out and thought about it for a moment, then decided against it. The break-up between them had been a bad one. Marie always had the way of making herself

™© *Z M Barrett*

the victim of whatever story she told, even if she wasn't the main focus. Of course, Spruyt wasn't blameless either. He'd lost the plot at the very end from what she'd heard. Beth did wonder if he'd been sectioned at some point but apparently, that was just a rumour spread in the 'spin war of the break-up,' she'd heard Spruyt had put it via Marie's other friends & acquaintances at the time.

Still, what happened was between them. Beth was in it for herself too, she thought, so this isn't an entirely selfless act. Life passes so quickly, situations change as do people. This was the now, the past didn't matter. On that mostly silent walk to his house, Beth pondered about telling Spruyt this.

She decided against it.

Spruyt was in his bathroom. The harsh tube lighting hid nothing. He'd emptied his bladder and washed his hands minutes ago. Yet, he was still there, staring at himself. At the mashed and wonky noise and the eyelid that droops slightly due to some dead nerve endings, the tiny scars in his stubble from his poor shaving skills and certain fights (they were hard to tell apart). Beth was better than this, Spruyt knew it. What is her endgame here? No, she's nicer than this. Than me. But then again-

And so it goes, battling himself for no other reason than the fact he'd met a person and not scared them away for a change. Acceptance can do strange things to the lonely and socially inept. The only thing that pulled Spruyt out of this endless circle of self-abuse was his deeply ingrained British politeness.

On his fourth or fifth cycle around the questioning of his situation, he suddenly realised he'd left Beth alone for way longer than was acceptable. Such poor hosting stills, so rude. On his way past his room, he stopped for a moment, then ducked inside. He retrieved a photo of himself next to some once-famous singer. It was a semi-popular band back when he was with Marie. She'd really liked them, as had Beth, one of the few things they connected over, from what Spruyt could tell. Beth had mentioned this at the bar when they were reaching for common ground.

™© *Z M Barrett*

He'd bought tickets for Marie as a gift. A birthday or something. Marie had taken the picture after she'd gotten her own. He chuckled as he thought about it. A couple getting a picture to keep with neither of them in the other one, a sign, clearly.

 Anyway, it was good; Spruyt needed an excuse for taking so long ('Sorry about that, I was just looking for this. I thought you'd get a kick out of it!') and Beth would enjoy the fact he'd spent time trying to find something to talk about, to keep the night going.

They got into bed. The duvet felt damp-cold to the touch as the heating hadn't been on. Holding each other felt nice. Spruyt was freaking out in waves; it'd retreat slowly then suddenly ramp up and smash into his consciousness. Like a tidal wave battering the shores during winds that would fade and come back without warning. The surf would be quiet then aggressive. No signs, no warnings, just boom. It wouldn't stop.

 Beth wanted him to kiss her, the wait causing an on-edge nervousness. He was too scared though. She could see it in his grey eyes, he wanted to cut this off before it got any deeper which could lead to more hurt. She felt the same, really. Still, it was nice just to be held, to float in the embrace of someone else. To know that at this very moment, in a universe so unforgiving and brutal, she was creating something nice. Beautiful, even. Connection of any kind always is. It doesn't matter if it lasts a minute, an hour or a year. When sharing joy together came, you took it. Wait a microsecond longer and it would evaporate into nothing but regret.

Spruyt was getting angry now. No, I won't let Maire control me anymore. I gave all that up. What am I doing, he thought, when a moment such as this has come along and I was letting my past, letting that bitch, take it away from me. This stops now.

He grabbed Beth's chin, tilted it up, and kissed her. Excitement grew within each of them.

She was lying on her side, facing away from him. He was on his back, staring up at that blank ceiling. It'd started well, *really* well, and it still wasn't enough. No feeling waist down, like his nerves had been shut off from the beltline. Shame and embarrassment were eating at him. Taking huge chunks of his self-confidence and self-worth and chewing on them like some fatty piece of meat. No, there was still time. This could be fixed. Screwing his eyes shut, he thought about Beth and what had started before. He felt some life, a little raise. Too right, he thought.

    Spruyt rolled onto his side and began to kiss Beth's neck. Slowly waking her from a light slumber, he wanted to do this properly.

It was a false-positive. A trick of hope, a trap of redemption. Spruyt rolled on his side away from Beth so she couldn't see his eyes. Silently, tears rolled down his face like thin blood pouring out of a shallow wound. It was bad, upsetting, but not life-threatening. Life-consuming, but not life-threatening.

Beth woke sometime after dawn. Momentarily, she clawed at her memories of the night before. She began pulling them up like polaroids from a file. She wasn't sure what this was but it had been nice. The only

Afterbirth

issue was the pain of failure in Spruyt's eyes. That was tough to see. It didn't matter to her that much. Sure, it was disappointing, but that's where it ended. It'll mean more to him though. Poor bloke, he's clearly still working through some stuff.

Silently, she got up and began to get dressed in the haze of dawn breaking into morning.

Spruyt woke with a start. Turning over, he caught Beth standing up fully dressed, tapping away at her phone. He wasn't sure if she'd noticed him yet. (She had, she was just busy getting transport sorted.) In his mind's-eye, he pictured her WhatsApp-ing all her girlfriends and ripping apart his (lack of) performance from last night. He wanted to say something. He couldn't.

Beth locked her phone and looked at Spruyt. 'Morning,' she said, that bitter taste of mortality on her tongue. Spruyt said nothing. His brain was a river. If he spoke, if he used his words, it'll all fall out of his mouth like a waterfall. Beth had been through enough already, he thought.

She said, 'Are you okay?'

™© Z M Barrett

Spruyt nodded in the affirmative. She smiled at this, bent down and kissed him on the forehead. Like a sick child, Spruyt thought. She got back up and turned to leave. As she walked away, Spruyt wanted to call out to her, to say goodbye. To ask her to call him. To make her promise, not just agree.

But he didn't. He'd embarrassed himself enough for one night.

Sleep wouldn't come. Neither would appetite or bowel/bladder movements. Spruyt just laid there, letting his own sadness warp his mind more. He put his weapons down at the gates and just let them in to run havoc.

He got up around mid-afternoon. Seeking out his phone, he knew nothing was waiting for him on it. Spruyt also knew he'd be waiting for contact from somebody that won't do it. He looked on at the spider-webbed cracked screen. If he didn't sort himself out, he'd be staring at it for hours. He shoved it down between the headboard and mattress where he'd found it before.

Pulling on some dirty boxers, he went downstairs. He checked the bottle of red from last night; empty. There was food in the house, plenty of it. But Spruyt had no need for it. What he wanted was an escape, not comfort. He pondered for a moment, wondering if they were the same thing but he soon binned this thought. He didn't want to fall down another rabbit hole. He'd been down far too many that morning already. He needed something, an event. Something time-consuming to focus on. A distraction that was within his humble means & surroundings. There was nothing else for it.

He went back upstairs and began to run a bath.

Stepping into the water, he let out a child's cry. High and pathetic. It was far too hot, like stepping into a just-boiled kettle. Marie's voice shot through his mind like a bullet, 'You can't do anything right, can you Paul? What are you even for, anyway?' Yeah, we'll see. He should have gotten out. He should have added cold water or something. But no, Spruyt decided it was a much better idea to battle the ghost voice inside his head. To stand against something that had already happened. He lowered himself down, slowly. The worst thing was the parts but this wasn't as bad as he thought it would be. His feet still throbbed with the heat, though.

Within minutes, his face was sodden. Not from the bathwater but his own acrid sweat. This, combined with the creeping burning sensation that was starting to crawl up his legs and thighs and arms, decided it for him. He splashed some water on his face to clear that thick sweat before getting out of the tub. His skin was lobster red. Sunburnt toast. Wrapping a towel around himself, he left the bathroom and went to lay down on his unmade bed.

As Spruyt lay there, he felt his entire body swell with heat. Even the towel that was wrapped around his legs and waist felt too close. His parts ached of lust, of his failure. Similar to toothache, it wasn't life-threatening but life-consuming.

Laying there, he could hear his own heartbeat in his ears. Looking down, he could see it pumping inside his chest. Ba-dum, ba-dum. All his ribs rattled with the effort. Spruyt looked on and thought, there it is, beating away with stubborn life. He wanted to get up after a while but couldn't; he felt faint. Light-headed. He closed his eyes and waited for it to pass.

A rapping at the door brought him back. He was downstairs, sat in the front room. He tried to form the how or why he was there but couldn't. Spruyt wasn't even sure if it was still the same day or the one after. It didn't seem to matter, anyway. As he got into the hallway the knocking sounded off again. It was a strong hand, backed by authority. Spruyt could picture the square-shaped wrist it was sat atop of. Before opening the door, he looked down to make sure he had trousers on. He had previous. Clocking the black tracksuit pants covered in lint and house dust, he nodded to himself and opened the door.
'Paulie! How's it cracking?'
Spruyt remained silent for a moment. His mind was blank as a piece of fresh paper.
'It's me, Thom? We used to work at Bennigan's?'

™© *Z M Barrett*

Cachi, Spruyt thought. He wasn't ready for this. Not now, Jebus, he thought. Save me, please!

'No, of course. What's up ma jigger?' Spruyt was talking mess, Thom was laughing politely. He probably didn't even know what a jigger was, Spruyt thought. For a split second, Spruyt dreaded that Thom had assumed he'd said the other word. The fact he was still wearing a forced smile after he finished laughing confirmed he hadn't. 'Come on in, Thom. Would you like a drink?'

'Coffee please, Paulie. Cheers.'

Bennigan's was from Spruyt's previous existence. Years he'd worked there and enjoyed it, too. He was good at it, or at least he thought he was. It'd never occurred to him to ask anyone else to validate this. Located in a quaint building outside the financial area of town, Bennigan's had been supplying the world with glass. To the manufacturers, really; lens for glasses, plains for windows, windshields for cars, sights for lasers and guns, all that. They made nothing here, that was up north somewhere. Spruyt couldn't

Afterbirth

recall whether it was based in Scotland or right on the board between the jocks and pale English. Spruyt helped sell and move the stuff around the world. He tried to stay clear of the military contracts if he could, something just didn't feel right about them.

Thom had worked with him in the same role. He was better at selling then he was at the logistic stuff. Since Spruyt's strengths lay in just that, they made a good team. Thom was that clean-cut poster boy all parents wanted their Jimmy or Andrew to grow into. Neat hair that never moved even in heavy wind, always clean shaved and dressed in tailored suits. He wasn't attractive in the average sense; his eyes were far too close to the bridge of his nose and his top lip was barely visible. It just looked like his skin stopped and his teeth started. Still, his confidence and elegant movement along with his drive and reliable nature took most people in. Including Spruyt, despite the fact, he didn't really engage with his type of humour. A nice guy is just that.

Spruyt returned with the two coffees. A black for him, a hispanic for Thom. It was touch-n-go whether the milk was usable but it passed a vigorous sniff test.

Again, relief shot through Spruyt at the relative cleanness of the house. Maybe that was the key, he pondered. He'd cleaned and in less than a week two people had visited, one had even stayed over. He shook that train of thought away from his head before it got any bigger or faster. Spruyt knew what he was like; if he let it continue it'd just crash & burn.

'So, how's things, Thom?' For some reason, Spruyt had addressed this to his mug and its contents, not Thom.

'Mate, it's bang-on; so much has changed since you left! Piney has gone now, finally retired. Sophie, you remember her? The one with the..?' At this, Thom made the shapes of two bowling balls at his chest, smiling like a teen seeing his first nipple. Spruyt tried to remember Sophie. She was a lovely girl, she really was, but she was known for what they called around the office 'her moments.' For example, Spruyt had once heard her say over the phone when trying to use the phonetic alphabet, 'Okay, so it starts with a "Q" for "cucumber."' Another time, when the power to the building cut out momentarily, she screamed. It was only out for a few seconds but her scream lasted the entire time the darkness was cast. When the power kicked back in, she stopped and looked last-minute-death-row-pardoned relieved. When Spruyt asked why she'd screamed, she told him she thought she'd gone blind.

Thom was still in fake-boob position as Spruyt reminisced. It looked bizarre, especially with the coffee mug in one hand. The mug Thom had was one Marie had brought him. A white mug, it had big bold black letters on it that said 'UNT.' The handle had been highlighted in black into the shape of a C too but most people missed this. Spruyt enjoyed the secret kick he got out of purposely giving the mug to any visitor that wanted a drink. When Marie gave it to him, she said, 'Look, I got you a mug with your name on it.'

Thom normally wasn't this full-on, from what Spruyt could remember, that is. Looking up from his own mug, he realised that with Piney and himself gone, that left an office full of women. An isolated man will use any opportunity to talk like a horn-heavy teenager with another bloke. Spruyt started to wonder whether he'd just come around to vent some of the male ego stupid-ness he couldn't use at work currently.

Finally, Spruyt replied to those big cans, 'Yeah.'

'Yeah you do! Anyway, she's gone too. Married and that now, sprogs running about and everything.' Thom took a pull from his coffee, that slurping sound was like nails on a chalkboard for Spruyt.

'Jebus man, do you kiss your mother with that mouth?'

Thom laughed. That wasn't meant to be funny, Spruyt thought.

'How are you doing anyway, Paulie?'

'Moodkee,' he said. Thom wasn't sure what this meant, whether it was good or bad. Spruyt knew this and left it at that.

Thom took another loud sip from his coffee. It sounded like someone ripping material. Spruyt used his own coffee as a screen of distraction, staring into the blank darkness of the drink, watching it give off steam into the air around him.

Afterbirth

The coffee felt hollow to Thom, flat. I've only tasted coffee like this once before, he pondered. Then he realised it was at Bennigan's when Spruyt worked there. The director of the business used to make a big deal about him re-brewing his used grounds, half-jokingly asking Spruyt if he paid him enough. Thom sensed it was nothing to do with money, it was Spruyt's warped sense of logic to do this. Thom didn't know why he knew this, he just did.

Alittle more silence passed. They both took another sip of the hollow coffee. Thom asked, 'are you still reusing your coffee grounds?'

'You know it, jigger.'

'You sensible maverick.'

Spruyt allowed himself a quiet chuckle at that. The term made absolutely no sense, it was perfect for him.

'I'll just come out and say it; I want you back.'

Spruyt stayed silent. Thom put the mug down next to his foot so he could use his hands as he spoke. If he'd stood up while doing this he would have looked like he was dancing. Or selling a timeshare or giving a TED talk.

'Listen, I know things have gone a bit… pete tong. I still don't understand why you quit in the first place, really.'

Thom waited for a response from Spruyt, both his hands frozen in mid-air as he waited. One was a little further in front of the other, the back of both hands facing Spruyt. Thom didn't get the response he waited for.

'So, anyway, with Piney gone and me moving up to middle-management, we need the manpower. They all still like you over there you know, Paulie. Even Sue and she hates everybody. Even me!' He laughed at himself, his eyes and smile portraying that how-is-that-even-possible kind of face.

'Thanks, Thom, I mean really. Thank you. It's just, it's so busy here you know, with little Michelle going to big school now, Dotty needing an on-call driver for all her piano lessons and socials, Larry needing me to be here when he gets home from school or he'll start tearing the plaster off the walls…you

Afterbirth

have kids, you know! I'm just not sure I'd have the time *to* work right now.'

Neither of them had kids. Whilst delivering this spiel, Spruyt had leaned back into the sofa. Both of his hands were still clasped around his mug. But somehow, his delivery had still been more energetic than Thom's. It all comes down to training, really. Thom had learnt to talk to people via coaching videos and training seminars. Spruyt had learnt in the field, putting himself out there and seeing what worked and what didn't. Why he seemed to pick what didn't work and run with that, only Spruyt would know. Thom chuckled but nervously so. Spruyt's type of humour had always left him a little lost.

Thom said, 'Dotty?'

'Dotty.'

He shook Spruyt's obtuse response away from his ears, why bother trying to understand, Thom thought, I just want the bloke to work for me, not make me laugh. He bent back down for his coffee, it was already lukewarm. Taking the necessary care to drink without noise, he chucked half of it down. He was leaving after the next few words so over

™© *Z M Barrett*

half the mug would have to have to be drained. It's just rude otherwise.

UNT, what a strange word, Thom thought. He reached for his inside pocket.

'Anyway, here's my new card. Both numbers are on there so you can get me whenever. When you are feeling up to it, give me a call. We can wait, but not too long.' Spruyt smiled as he nodded. He's a good man really, he thought. And I still treated him like a numpty. Spruyt soon realised that showed more about him then it did about Thom.

'Thanks,' Spruyt responded.

Thom got up to leave, saying it was good to see him and the house in better shape (he'd called once before, it'd be an adventure. That's the most polite way of putting it) and asked him to call him about the job or if he needed anything else. Spruyt showed him out. Just as they got to the door, Thom asked,

'UNT...is that Welsh or something?'

'Gaelic, actually.'

'Ah, right,' Thom responded, impressed. He went on, 'What does it mean?'

Spruyt held Thom's gaze for a moment. Was he being funny or genuine? He couldn't

Afterbirth

tell. The poor guy is just trying to help me, Spruyt pondered, connect with me on a normal level. A moronic comment was lurking in his throat but he swallowed it back. It tasted like battery acid, burning as it went down. Eventually, Spruyt answered.

'It means "hero," Thom. Thanks again for popping by.'

'No worries amigo, keep that double-chin up.' Thom shut the door behind him. Spruyt let out a small, laboured cough.

On returning the mugs to the kitchen sink, Spruyt found himself pulling Thom's card out from his pocket. Why he'd quit was because of Marie. After everything that happened, he just didn't want to go back in. Partly because the reason he held that job was to support their home & life together. Secondly, he was too embarrassed to go back. They all knew what'd happened. Spruyt wasn't strong enough to face that.

So, he quit. He went on pause, a break from living how he should and proceeded to see how it would be if he lived in a hole. A void. So far, overall, it wasn't so great.

™© *Z M Barrett*

Sleeping in until noon most days, being in your own space and not feeling on show, yeah, that was pretty sweet. The novelty had soon worn off for him though, and now he felt trapped. He couldn't be out there but he couldn't be in here either. So, like many before him and many will after, he turned to Dr ink. DRINK. It wasn't a release, it was a straightjacket. It got you away from yourself for a period of time, yes, but when you came back you felt just as worse. Lugging yourself and that horrible hangover around, clinging to your back like a monkey or sitting on your shoulders like an uncouth parrot was both physically and emotionally draining.

    Spruyt was still looking at Thom's card. His hand began to shake. He wanted to bin the card, badly. Despite the longing for something to change, to get better, he was still unsure he wanted it. The grass is always greener. Deceitful too, the power of landscaping. Anyway, he pulled himself together with some loose strings of reason. He turned around and stuck the card behind a magnet on the fridge. The magnet he chose was the one holding up a picture of himself

Afterbirth

and Marie at some park somewhere. The card was now covering Marie's face.

He crushed the can. The dregs of the washback dribbled down his hand alittle. It looked like a frisbee now, a very jagged frisbee. Spruyt threw it into the recycling sack. He picked up a pen and added it to the tally he was keeping. He was on one hundred and forty-two now, the sack wasn't even half full yet. Progress.

His phone bleeped. Sitting on the can, Spruyt wondered if it was worth reading. He'd emptied his bowels some time ago. He was just sitting there now. Like it was his throne. It certainly felt like the right place for him to sit, that was for sure.

Spruyt's heart tried to jump out of his chest when he did check it. It was Beth. That was all he knew, all he wanted to know. Under her name, it read she'd sent him one message. He wanted to hold on to this feeling for as long as he could. The message could contain anything, a schrodigender's text, and he didn't

™© *Z M Barrett*

have the balls to check it. He didn't have the balls to do a lot of things, recently.

He was now cleaning his teeth. It'd been some time since he had last done them and they felt like itchy moss, so Spruyt had gone in for a real sesh. He must've been six minutes deep by this point. Remaining in the house they'd shared together, he struggled to escape the past. It lurked everywhere. Spruyt found himself in an endless game of hide-and-seek with memories he'd rather he didn't have. He could have moved, sure. But all that paperwork, searching for a new place, packing up his stuff, changing the bills, all that malarkey, it was just easier to stay. In the physical sense, anyway.

Spruyt was really digging into his mouth now. His dentist had told him years ago to ease up on the power. 'You'll end up taking off all your enamel, son.' Still, he brushed away. The whole purpose of brushing your teeth was to keep them healthy, Spruyt thought, and only I could somehow turn brushing into a bad thing. Sickly white paste spluttered everywhere. The wall, the mirror, the sink. It was all pebble-dashed with it.

    Marie had been using the toilet, that time. Way back when. Or the sink, Spruyt couldn't remember. Years they'd been together when this happened. All those years and she still hated sharing the bathroom. There was only one in the house. The spare room downstairs was going to be converted, they'd decided. Well, Marie had decided. Families should share things in Spruyt's opinion. The dinner table, the sofa, the bathroom, it'll all provide memories for the retirement home. Anyway, he tried his luck. He walked in and picked up his toothbrush. Cue yelling, get out, yadda yadda. Laughing, Spruyt picked up the toothpaste and squeezed a bud onto his frayed brush. Which was a skill in itself. Instead of pointing straight up, his bristles tended to point at a forty-five-degree angle.

    Leaving the bathroom and walking down the narrow stairs, he started cleaning his teeth. He'd do that a lot, walk around the house while brushing. Barely using a mirror. A minor quirk or a serious concern, who knows.

™© *Z M Barrett*

He went into the kitchen to use that sink. He spat out his dregs and carried on. Spruyt's mind wandered, his eyes closed. Zone of Zen during a slow weekend morning. He spat out the last of the mess and cleaned the brush. He swilled his mouth out, job done. He returned his brush to the bathroom when it was free. That should be the end of the story, right? Nah.

Later, Marie was making her lunch. Who knows what Spruyt was up too. Her mind was racing a mile-a-minute. She wasn't towing her five-year plan. The marriage and kids were missing, a year late *already*. The only reason they had the house was because it had been left to them by Spruyt's grandmother. God bless that woman, Marie thought, she'd tried. She'd seen her, countless times, screaming at Spruyt. Like Marie, his Nan was driven, logical and thorough. Not Spruyt, he had a real lazy streak in him. Often, he'd wander away in the meadow of his mind and get lost there. 'Away with the fairies,' his Nan often called it. Marie knew this all too well. All she, and his Nan really, wanted was for him to do things to the best of his ability

Afterbirth

all the time. All Spruyt wanted…well, it was just that. He didn't want anything. He was happy just staring out of the front window people watching or laughing through a kaleidoscope or asking Marie stupid questions like 'Would you rather have no fingers or no toes?'

The poor woman had tried. It'd been passed onto Marie now to beat this immature streak out of him. Cleaning the house was 'pointless,' reading up on the best way to clean windows was a 'waste of time' to Spruyt, he'd just attack them with a dishcloth, Windolene and a polishing cloth. This far in, Marie was mentally drained. She loved him, but she was starting to feel mugged off. Used. She signed up for the happy-ever-after, not to be a carer.

Anyway, back to this distant lunch. She was making a tuna mayo sandwich on rye beard. Taking care of yourself was important, she often told Spruyt that whilst he was on his third cup of coffee. 'Just let me live my life, please,' he'd say. There won't be much left of one if he kept that diet up, she would often think.

™© *Z M Barrett*

The five-year plan was heavy in her mind. Slapping on the filling, Marie noticed a white spot on the floor. She cursed at herself. How stupid, she thought, and what a waste of good mayo. She crouched down and swiped it up with her finger. Several moments later, she stood there. Staring at the white blob on the tip of her index finger. Why not, she thought. No one will know. She put the blob in her mouth and tasted nothing but the viscous mint of toothpaste.

That did it.

She flew into a rage, screaming words. Well, maybe words. It wasn't just this though; it'd been years of this sort of stuff. She'd dammed it off in her mind, letting the stupid things Spruyt did build and build and build. Now, that dam had burst. The villagers of this relationship were in trouble. What's worse, she couldn't find him in the house. He was in what they used as the spare room (presently his bedroom) pissing about with boxes of stuff he'd promise he'd clear when they moved in. He spent more time in that part of the house than anywhere else. Surrounded by his childhood things. It was sad. She ran around the ground floor, nothing. Storming up the stairs, Spruyt considered closing the door and holding it shut. Marie had always had a temper. This didn't stop him from leaving windows open or toothpaste everywhere or only sweeping half the floor. He decided to take his punishment as he'd earned it.

It wasn't enough, though. As Marie screamed her point at him, she knew it wouldn't get through. In their early days, he used to nod and say the right things. Now, he stayed silent. Spruyt himself was sick of the same conversations or arguments about his behaviour but he was trapped in it like a whirlpool. Around and around he went, doing the same stupid things. Marie needed this to land, she wasn't spending the rest of her life like this. Red in the face, eyes ablaze with white-hot rage, she let her body show her feelings. It was the only thing she had left.

She slapped him, hard. Right across his stupid face. Spruyt didn't fall, but he felt like his neck almost snapped. His face burned with the pain and shame of what had just happened. Marie felt awful, she wanted to cry. To ball like a child. To hug him and say sorry.

™© *Z M Barrett*

Spruyt wanted to cry too. He was lost in the situation along with her. But they both just stood there under the weight of what had just happened. What they had both witnessed, what they had both been a part of.

Presently, Spruyt spat out the last of his toothpaste. With it, he tried to spit out that memory of Marie and the first time it happened. It didn't work. He cleaned up and went downstairs. Stopping at the living room door, he let his head drop for a moment. He had on his Stan Smiths, a somewhat respectable Fred Perry knock-off, a pair of jeans and had showered yesterday. For a split-second the side of his face, the same side Marie had hit all those memories ago, burned up. Spruyt lifted his head and saw his jacket on the peg by the door. He grabbed it on his way out of the house.

It only got worse from then. Walking through the cold streets, flashes of horrible things came back to Spruyt. After the first time, they talked into the night, trying to piece things back together. It sounded good at the time.

Afterbirth

Spruyt promised to be better, to be more aware and try to care more about the little things. Marie promised to control her temper and not make mountains from molehills. Changing is the easy part, making it last is the problem.

A few more slaps followed. Spruyt wasn't intentionally thoughtless, he was just more concerned about the contents of his own head than what went on around him. To Marie, intent didn't matter. If you split your drink, you split it. It doesn't matter if the glass you had suddenly cracked or someone pushed you. The drink had been split. End of.

In regards to thought-process, they spoke *completely* different languages to each other. Sometimes this complements a relationship and fits together like a jigsaw, other times...

Clearly, the slaps weren't working. He was still leaving bits on the dishes and spots of piss on the bathroom floor.

Soon, Marie graduated into fists.

The first time she broke his nose, Spruyt felt nothing emotionally. He was just numb. At work, the way he re-told it made it sound like they were play-fighting, as young-in-love couples do and he caught one. The second time it was a fight in the pub. Friends and co-workers believed this, after all, they knew Spruyt couldn't help himself. A smart mouth leads to challenges.

The third time, Spruyt didn't have the effort to come up with a story.

The thing that scared him most about all this was that he'd caused it. By simply being himself, he'd turned a loving woman and potential mother to his children into a complete wrecking ball of rage & violence.

Marie decided she was addicted. It was like a drug, in a way. The violence. It gave you a comedown/hangover worse than any drug or drink out there. But, before this, there was a rush. Imposing yourself like that helped. It released all that five-year plan stress, those stupid office politics, that jealously of friends, those missed milestones. She'd long given up on changing Spruyt. She needed to change herself now, she'd taken a road that was scary to be on. And hard to get off.

Spruyt was now at a cashpoint. Man, the funds were low. When had he last got his grino? He wasn't sure, exactly. Still, he needed to get out of his head. It was taking him back into the horribleness of what it had seen. Fifty should do it. Thank god for overdrafts.

Marie loved her TV. Often, Spruyt would find her slumped in front of the iPlayer or Netflix or Prime. Watching the latest series, boning up on all the latest social and economic issues. Watching her beloved team, wasting hours upon hours invested on the shiny bright lights and all the movement they contained. Not for him, Spruyt knew. He was too focused on the pictures going on in his head to focus on the ones from the TV.

  She sat like a man. Spruyt would often tease her for this. Back slumped so far down it was almost level with the seat cushion. Both legs wide apart, planted as far as they could get away from each other, groin out to the world. He often sat crossed legged. It was weird to look at them when they were both sitting in the same room.

™© *Z M Barrett*

Anyway, Spruyt doesn't know when but at some point he knew that was the key. If things ever went too far (hadn't they already?!?) that was his in. The TV. Money in the bank, he darkly thought to himself.

He was four ales in now, the numbness was starting. He felt a stupid smile spread across his stupid face. It was poorly lit, the shadows outshining the lights. He'd managed to get a bar stool which was good, his dogs were barking. Looking around, Spruyt took the others in. He could be anyone, now. What must they see, he thought. Perspective, that old chestnut. Was it a given, or did you have to earn it? The ale addled brain of Spruyt thought this was an epiphany. When you lived inside your head as much as he did, anything remotely avant-garde felt like a breakthrough. He felt a nudge in his back, some bloke had just fallen into him.

'Brussels! How's it haggling?'

Spruyt turned around, he had no idea who this was. He simply raised his glass in acknowledgement. He was still wearing that stupid smile.

Afterbirth

'Is right, is right! How's the bird?' Really, Spruyt thought, straight to that? It's the reaching of the common ground again. He's only trying to make conversation. Still, Spruyt thought, it felt like he was asking how's the limp after having one of your legs removed.

'Locked and loaded. She's in the gimp mask back home, waiting for me.'

'You sick puppy! I remember when she gave you that black eye and bust nose, you pair must be into some crazy shit. Is right, is right!' Not for the first time, the bartender came to Spruyt's rescue. Jebus, who is this guy? Spruyt didn't want to start anything but he could feel himself going wonky. Any more of this and he'll be squaring up head-to-head with this bloke whilst saying some very unpleasant things about his mother.

The bloke ordered two pints. Spruyt pretended to check his phone whilst the guy waited for his drinks. Beth's message was still unread. Still with schrodigender's cat. He felt a sharp pain in his thumb, a spec of glass had come free again from the cracked screen. Spruyt put his phone away and tried to stem the bleeding by sucking his thumb. The bloke

™© *Z M Barrett*

turned around at this point to say something but seeing Spruyt as he was, he just started laughing. With his free hand, Spruyt made a faux gun out of his index finger and thumb and pointed it to his own temple with humour in his eyes. Still laughing, the bloke turned back around to the bar to finish up with his order. As he did this, Spruyt dropped the humour from his gaze and pointed the gun at the back of the bloke's head instead. He was still sucking his cut thumb like a child as he did this. As the bartender came back with the drinks he caught Spruyt's gaze. Looking directly into his eyes, Spruyt mimicked pulling the trigger.

    Money was exchanged over the bar, Spruyt dropped both his hands to his sides. He needed to make his wayonnaise out of this place after his oddball actions. Before he could bail, the bloke turned and said,

    'This is for you Sprouty, keep on slaying it brother!'

    'I will, jigger, I will.'

    That was the last thing Spruyt needed. After his weird actions, he couldn't stay here now. That bartender looked freaked out. But

Afterbirth

he'd been tricked by the free drink. It's almost like the bloke knew what he was doing. Revenge is a dish best served ignorant.

    Well, you reap what you so, Spruyt pondered.

Where now, Spruyt thought. He was feeling claustrophobic. All the pubs/bars within his safe zone were binned. They offered nothing, zip. His legs knew where he was going before he did. Spruyt took a sharp right and was basked in a sickening glow. It was the harsh lighting of the train station. He reached into his front pocket, he crinkled the plastic notes inside it. There were at least three in there, plus a clunk of weighty change.

    A ride into town? 'Why not,' Spruyt said to no one.

It wasn't only the TV. Marie also loved this hideous pink fluffy tutu. Growing up, her parents did the usual gender power play. When she kicked a ball they'd grab it and change it for a doll. When Marie asked for a new galactic starship complete with laser cannons and ejectable figures ('for real live-action movement whilst playing!') they smiled smugly and gave her a new EZ bake oven instead. Imagine her surprise, when on the morning of her twelfth birthday, Marie unwrapped a makeup kit and several summer dresses after she'd asked several times for her team's latest football jersey. She'll grow out of it, Marie's parents knew, it was just a phase.

    It was, obviously, who she was. Who she *is*. Out of all this power play, for some reason, this tutu stuck. It no longer fitted Marie but she kept it anyway. Secretly, she knew it was because it was the one thing her parents had brought her which she liked. She couldn't explain it, on paper with everything she is as a person and her individuality, she should've hated this thing. But she didn't. And it was her one link to her parents, a time where they were all on the same page, a happy family.

    Spruyt knew this too. Like everyone else in Marie's life, he pestered her about it. She didn't break at first. During one of Spruyt's mad fits of trying to be productive, he went through their shared wardrobe and decided this tutu was taking up space that was required. 'Why is this on the bed?' Spruyt looked up and told her, 'It's to be thrown out. It's too small for you now anyway, what's the point of keeping it?' Marie jumped forward onto the tutu and hugged it like a life jacket that had just been thrown to her whilst drowning in a cold sea. So, she told him. Explained everything to Spruyt, why it was important to her.

    This came to Spruyt's mind on the day his control imploded.

He wasn't sure whether he was swaying because of the train or the ale. Spruyt felt like a palm tree, gently falling to one side, halting suddenly, then retreating back up to only fall away to the opposite side. There was a hubbub brewing several seats behind him, he could hear it. He could feel it. The dialect was hard, biting. It was a group of Scottish lads. Spruyt tried to pin down in his mind which part of Scotland but the sloshing of the ale in his blood and brain made this impossible.

    The sounds of a scuffle were echoing through the carriage, accompanied by 'Nah, Nah' coming from someone in between burps.

™© *Z M Barrett*

Closing his eyes, Spruyt could picture it, four or six lads sat next to each other, spread across two sets of the four seats, one of the lads trying to get up with the other three/five each grabbing an arm or shoulder to push him back down onto his vacant seat. The ale goggles were on, blocking all reality out and only leaving fears and blurs. Spruyt was laughing at himself, at the scene in his head. He was also trying to mask his nervousness. Anything could happen on the train to town, ninety-four per cent of passengers had already had a skin full. A small part of Spruyt was concerned about the problem that the lad had was with *him*. He was like a dog in that way, Spruyt; if he was scared he'd lash out at the source before they could strike first, despite not having the fight to back it up. The lad trotted up the carriage and came within earshot of Spruyt,

'Nah, Nah, come at me.'

'What's that boss?' Spruyt hated himself, he couldn't just leave it. It was too difficult for him to stay quiet, coast through whatever this was.

'Awright, ye hear me?'

Afterbirth

Spruyt opened his eyes and turned around. The lad was heavily kitted out in Adidas; green gazelles, a black & white track hoody and a red baseball cap. All were boasting the striped logo in some way making it look like the brand had vomited up on him. No hair was peeking out of the hat, just head stubble. The lighting of the train made it look a light grey. Only his boot cut jeans were standard, brandless. He had both his hands up in weak fists, the thumb and fingers barely closed over. He too was swaying. His eyes seemed half-closed like he'd fallen asleep and his eyelids had started to fall open, like old people's do when they nap in the day chair. The rest of the group was a dark smudge behind the lad, their laughing creeping through the air. Spruyt held his gaze to the red hat from his seat, he was ready to stand up and say something stupid.

'Ye hear me? A fucking *hate* hedgehogs. Come at me, ya jabby wee cunt.' The lad started to circle around something that was on the floor just to the side of Spruyt. Turning full De Niro with his squint, Spruyt bent forward to try and see what it was. When the

™© *Z M Barrett*

scales of ale cleared from his vision, Spruyt saw what it was. It was a brown hairbrush that had been dropped spikes up. The lad went too far to the left and fell into all four vacant seats over from Spruyt. The smudge of the lads' friends behind him burst out into a full stand-up comedy crowd laugh.

Spruyt let out a small, laboured cough.

'Arms out like this please, mate,' the bouncer signalled. Spruyt assumed that this is what he said, based on the fact that when he walked up to him he lifted his arms out Christ-on-the-cross style. His mouth moved and Spruyt placed these words in his voice. He was going to pat him down, clear him as safe. Check if I'm safe, Spruyt thought, why is it a given that *he* is safe? Just because he works here. As the bouncer, with his slicked-back ponytail, pen marker straight-trimmed beard and permanent scowl, held out his arms to demonstrate what he wanted Spruyt to do, he decided to take this chance and knelt down and patted the bouncer's legs and arms. Feeling the heavily insulated coat as he replicated the motions that the bouncer wanted to do, he touched either his wallet or hip flask on his inner right-hand side pocket and said, 'What's this?'

Stupefied, the bouncer tried to say what? but was cut off again by Spruyt before he could reply. 'I'm just joshing,' Spruyt said, 'You're okay, amigo.'

Walking down the steps into the place, the bouncer managed to regain his composure in time and grabbed Spruyt around the right shoulder. He spun him around on his heel and cursed. Spruyt threw his hands up in surrender and smiled as this happened. He didn't fight the motion, he just let himself be moved by the ponied-bouncer's action. When he had Spruyt facing the street again, he brought his free hand up alongside the one he already had on Spruyt and shoved him hard back onto the street.

Amongst the laughter and on my god's from the queue behind him, Spruyt took a gentleman's bow (right arm across the chest, left arm stuck out and legs steel-straight as he lowered himself from the waist) before he moved on.

™© *Z M Barrett*

He was in another bar now. What was the difference between a pub and a bar? Spruyt had no idea. Was it just an American-ism or was there a genuine difference? He hated all that. Like 'good morning,' it was always a *good* morning in the States. Here, it was just morning. We aren't more cultured than them, Spruyt thought, we're just realists. Not every morning is good. Just saying it's good doesn't make it so. Things happen, some days are battles. Others, wars. The odd few are parades. The Ying and yang, the up and down, like a mountain plain. Days are varied and saying good morning…it makes every day so flat.

    See, this is what Spruyt had to deal with. His mind was like a young puppy let off its lead in a vast grassy park or moor. It was just gone, chasing strange threads of thought. Whilst all this was going on, toothpaste was getting dropped on the floor, piss was getting left on the toilet seat, dust from the floor was just being moved about instead of swept up and binned. In Spruyt's world, focus didn't exist. It was a fairy, a leprechaun, a dragon, justice. Something make-believe, anyway.

Afterbirth

He'd planted himself at the bar for two reasons; one, as he was on his own he had no one to talk to. Two, he needed the support. The pre-town ales had hit him hard, knocking him wonky. He didn't want a drink and was grateful the place was busy. Spruyt was trying to use this as camouflage. He stood there, vacant.

How much time passed, who knows. The bartender in front of Spruyt didn't bark a question at him as most in her profession did. She'd learnt the power of eye contact. When the music system was blaring, words were useless. A wave of people had come in with the trains (Spruyt being one of them) so she'd spent the past twenty minutes or so pinging from one punter to another, serving drinks as fast as her small hands would allow. The herd had thinned out, retreated to the dancefloor or the booths or the smoking garden, and there was Spruyt. She couldn't tell from his face whether he would moan about the wait or jump when he thought the pumps were staring at him.

Spruyt had seen her query via the eyes and he waited as long as he could. He spotted a long intertwining mess of tattoos down her exposed right arm. He couldn't make out what they were meant to be, they just looked like lines and shapes from a colouring book. She was burning into his head with that stare, he had to say something.

'Nice sleeve.'

'Oh, thanks,' She couldn't be arsed with this. I should just pick up my phone, she thought, and tweet to the entire world, *Step off; live your life, not your desires*. She made a mental note to write that down before her shift ended; it could go viral. She waited for an order that did not come. Again, she fired a question at Spruyt with her eyes.

'You look like a page from a colouring book. Have you ever been tempted to colour them in with a sharpie? I would have.' What was I talking about, Spruyt thought. Just get the drink and nurse it like a man. She pulled a smile with her mouth only, not her eyes. It looked painful, like a grimace. Like a week-old Halloween jack-o-lantern.

'Yeah, sorry; I'll have a vodka and whisky please.'

Afterbirth

Spruyt hadn't caught what he'd said, not at first. She did, of course, and let herself laugh a little. This guy was on one, she pondered. Slowly, it dawned on Spruyt what he'd said. Even so, like most men his age, his gender too actually, he was too proud to say otherwise. He was committed now, he knew, so that was that.

She replied, 'Do you mean a vodka and lemonade?'

'I know what I said.'

Someplace else now. The bridges in the last place had been burnt quite drastically with Spruyt's rambling nonsense. Again, he was propping up the bar. This time he'd committed to the drink straight away so there would be no interruptions, no demands, no pressure. He was out of notes now, so options were threadbare. Home wasn't a viable option either, Spruyt wanted to be beyond-gone before he returned to that sneering shadow of a house.

The music was low in this place like it was an afterthought. Spruyt preferred it. Every other place he'd been in up to that point was blaring music like an explosion. Like it was a crime not to fill every free space of the place with sound. Quiet places were better for alone drinking, Spruyt thought, it meant you could geg-in on conversations. Listen to something close by which made you feel included. It also meant you didn't have to offer anything, just take. Spruyt enjoyed that.

For example, he knew the bloke standing next to him right now was called Mark. Some tub of lard with no neck and a forehead melted with wrinkles had been taking the mick out of him about some football thing. A result, Spruyt assumed. He never watched the sport himself, not anymore. The repetitive motion of the out-field players moving back & forth looking for an opening like a lifesize game of chess, with the ineligible yelling and passion of a religious sermon was too much for him. The investment of your emotion cost more than he was willing to spend.

Anyway, Spruyt was glad he now had a name to put to the face. Mark was upsetting Spruyt. Had he barged or pushed into him? Nope. Had he been rude or insulting? Nada.

Afterbirth

Had he looked at him with a side-eye or spilt his drink or slagged off his religion or called him a karen? None of the above. It was something much more pettier.

How dare he, Spruyt thought, how *dare* he stand there with his perfectly sculpted blonde hair, big hulking shoulders and a litheness in the rest of his body, with a well-fitted suit of dark navy, being all that a woman wants. He's the kind of lad that would be better for Beth then me, he would've kept his own with Marie too. Made sure he stood his ground not shrivelled like a chocolate bar wrapper in a fire like I did, Spruyt thought. Internally, he was yelling these thoughts at himself. His face had crumpled into an ugly mask of vexation. The spit in his mouth was drying into a horrible thick white paste of aggression.

'Mark,' Spruyt said.

The big hunk turned, saw Spruyt and was immediately on guard. What does this loon want?

'Yeah?'

'I have a question...Mark.' Spruyt thought he was being super clever with this.

It's fair to say, even a sober comedian would struggle to follow his sideways humour.

Mark replied, 'What's that?'

Spruyt remained silent with a sickly grin on his face. He looked like a month old party balloon. What's this guy's problem, Mark thought, I'm in no mood for this. Tony has already ripped the piss out of me for the result last night, now I've got this loon trying to crackwise. Mark was scared of Spruyt a little but that was only due to his appearance. He looked like he didn't have much to lose, this joker, which could make him capable of anything. Finally, Spruyt offered some sort of response. He said,

'Look at ya, all smiles and percocet. I bet you're the kind of guy that brushes his teeth with warm water, aren't ya? The kind of guy that lands on a round number at the petrol pump *without* even trying,' Spruyt quickly turned & down ¾ of his drink before turning back to continue on ale stained breath, 'ya'know, the kind of mook that follows ready meal instructions like the gospel of the working middle-class?'

'Listen, pal, you got a problem?'

Afterbirth

Yeah, Spruyt thought, I've got a problem. I've got several of the pricks, actually. He turned to face this Mark again and felt the tension in the air. He enjoyed holding onto it, seeing him ready for action. He was ready to throw down, Spruyt could see that. The tension between them was peaking, it felt like the air was sweating. He was ready to strike but Spruyt was about to throw him a curveball. Jerking his upper body alive, Spruyt's hands suddenly reached across to Mark whilst saying, 'This is a nice tie, is it Ted Baker?'

Mark sprung into action, misreading (as Spruyt intended) the action as a punch or an attempt at a headbutt. He caught him before he grabbed his tie and threw his arms away. Where the hell is that server, Mark pondered. Spruyt pulled his arms back in and folded them across his chest. He rested one of his elbows on the bar as he faced Mark. As he watched the momentary panic drain out of his eyes, Spruyt spat out 'Why so narky, Marky?'

'You seem to know my name, pal, so what's yours?'

'Paul.'

™© *Z M Barrett*

He was still smiling as he waited for Mark's response. He was hoping it'd be physical, he wanted punching out of this numbness. The sedation of the ale was heavy in his head. Blurring out all emotions, good and bad. A mental static. It wasn't just that, his body felt it too. The numbness was weighing all his limbs down like wet clothes. Here it comes, he thought.

'Paul, you're a dickhead.'

'Yeah,' Spruyt replied as he slowly turned back to his low drink.

He fell into the door. Spruyt wanted to know what the time was but it didn't occur to him to ask anyone or check his phone. He just let himself ponder on the endless possibilities on what time it *could* be. He could just solve all his problems right now by asking, he just didn't have the courage to do so.

He straightened himself out then grabbed each side of his jacket like an old-timey lawyer from the wild kanye west. Fists on his chest, elbows pointed drastically to the floor. Spruyt made his way to the shiny counter. The guys serving knew he'd be a

Afterbirth

flight risk but it'd been a slow night, they needed the footfall and what little business he would bring. Spruyt's manner & dress code screamed a bargain box glass ceiling to those behind the till.

'Yes, boss?'

Spruyt brought his right hand up to his chin and pulled his mouth up in an expression of deep thought.

'Tell me, fair representative of this fine delicatessen, how much is it for a piece of fried chicken?'

'Two-fifty, boss.' Spruyt nodded his head slowly in acknowledgement. It had already been a long night for the guys behind the counter, and with this conversation beginning, it was starting to feel a lot longer.

'So riddle me this, amigo; how much would it be for **two** pieces of the same said chicken?' The server paused for a minute, trying to see if Spruyt was joking or not. He was not.

'Five,' he said.

Spruyt slammed his right hand down on the counter with a brutal force. Even the guys deep inside the kitchen and behind the fryer

jumped. Spruyt locked eyes with the server and bore into his vision like his life depended on it. Eventually, he said,
'You sir, have yourself a deal.'

He felt like he was on the train again. Swaying, uneven in his steps. As he walked past a changing traffic light, another mocking amber smiley face shone down on him again. Spruyt went to take another bite of his food but only found an empty styrofoam container sweating droplets of geese at the bottom of it. He binned it when he could, in case he fell for that again. His stomach was screaming at him, it wasn't happy. Growling and roaring like bad plumbing, it made known sharpish it was bouncing its food back for the bad cheque it was. Spruyt brought up a fist as some vomit came up. He coughed it back down but he knew it was a token effort. Taking a sharp left into a suspect alley off the main street, he made no effort to fight the second coming.

The first few heaves were chunky and hurt his throat, the rest was mainly a muddy liquid. Spruyt felt better, at first. That was until he caught sight of some of the

Afterbirth

regurgitated chicken; it looked no different from when he ate it mere minutes ago. This sparked off another round of painful and somewhat dry heaving.

The driver shook his head. Who in this day and age, he thought, paid their bus fare with coins. The risk it posed since that rona debacle…He knew better than to ask if he had a mask with him. True, it was only optional these days, but it was a force of habit for him now to ask. One of the many mental ticks left from what happened during all that.

    He was binned this cat, the driver thought, as Spruyt stood at his air-brake hissy door. It wasn't worth the hassle, trying to stop him from getting on. He'd only get himself in trouble left in town anyway, the driver reasoned with himself. He prayed to karma that since he'd had this thought, Spruyt would return the favour and not cause him any trouble either. Be arsed with a throwout tonight. The driver's back was already tingling with an ache at the mere thought of having to be called into action.

™© *Z M Barrett*

Spruyt was counting out the money, slowly. It was only a one-way ticket he needed but he'd blasted through his funds like a masturbating teenager through a box of kleenex. Finally, he paid up. Taking his ticket out of the machine, he retreated to the back of the bus.

He had no recollection of choosing a seat, he just found himself sitting down. There weren't many people on the bus, Spruyt could see at least two different blurs within the seats in front of him. His throat felt scratchy and his head was thick with exhaustion. A wave of panic hit him as he thought about his phone, he hadn't seen it in a while. Thumping his jean pockets only exasperated his panic, it wasn't there. It was just a phone, it wasn't the end of the world, but to Spruyt it felt differently. He *needed* that phone, he had unfinished business.

    'Where's my phone?' he blurted out to no one. His frantic patting of pockets had reached his jacket now. No, no, *crunch*. There it was, Spruyt heard the thud and cracking of the phone screen. I never use my inside pocket, Spruyt pondered, why is it there?

Afterbirth

'Found it!'

'Pardon?' it was a delicate voice and it was close. Spoken so softly that it demanded your attention. Spruyt looked around and saw a woman, possibly a girl she was that small, seated (maybe) few rows in front of him. She was wearing a baby-blue surgical mask that hid her nose and mouth. Her eyes were an electric-light blue, intense like lightning. The black hair was cropped short into a bob, the fridge diagonal across her wrinkle-free forehead. Spruyt was out of words, out of effort. He dropped his head down while laughing to himself. The half-face asked again what he'd said.

'Nothing, I just found my phone,' he slurred in reply. Her eyebrows arched and eyes narrowed in suspicion. 'I thought I'd lost it. Turns out I have too many pockets. # first world problems and that.'

'You should have a mask on.'

'Hmm?'

'I said you should have a mask on, I have a spare one, I think.'

™© *Z M Barrett*

Spruyt shook his head and raised his hands, 'Jigger, please. It's okay, it'd be wasted on me anyways.'

'Oh, it's fine; they are so cheap now. I even got given this one for free, it's in here somewhere...' She'd started feverishly looking through her handbag.

'Honestly, it's fine.'

'Don't worry about-'

'Like I said,' his voice was loud now, soaked with anger and protest, 'it'd be wasted on me.' Spruyt wanted to say he wasn't worth saving, but even in his drunken state, it still sounded way too pathetic to say out loud.

Half-mask stopped her searching and remained dumbfounded at Spruyt. What is this guy's problem, she thought. I'm just trying to help and he shouts at me. She remained focused on him as he swayed slightly. Even when the bus stopped, he was swaying. Spruyt was just waiting for it. The insult or the yelling back. When it didn't come, he thought he'd wave his white flag of apology. The words didn't come, though. They were lost to the ages like the city of Atlantis.

Afterbirth

As half-mask turned around, she whispered, 'Dickhead.'

Spruyt let out a small, laboured cough.

Well, Spruyt thought, I'd made it home. There is a victory in that, somewhere. He'd woken with a start, a harsh inhale of cold damp air. Since then, he'd just laid on the sofa, shivering. His jacket and shoes were straddled across the floor at unholy angles. Some sense must have reached him when he walked in and faced the old steep and narrow staircase. Deciding to sleep on the sofa showed Spruyt was still able to demonstrate common sense, at least occasionally.

Berating himself into moving, Spruyt sat up. Sloth slow, he swung his legs off the sofa and placed them on the floor as lightly as possible. He held his forehead in one of his hands, the palm feeling the heavy sweat that was sitting there. Beads of it like the skin of a basketball, they sank of stale ale. His tongue felt like a sundried piece of leather, stretched taut and useless in his mouth. Images of the night before dropped in flashes behind his eyes; antagonising strangers, spending money he didn't have, making a general berk of himself. The shivering of his soul sent out shockwaves through the rest of his body.

    The hangover was back, sitting heavy on his shoulders. Its hands were battering Spruyt around his head whilst its legs kicked its heels into his stomach & aching guts. Just holding himself sat up, Spruyt was struggling. He could feel Atlas shrugging. Jumping like he'd been shot, Spruyt grew angry with himself. It was only a phone ringing, he thought. He reached over from the sofa to his jacket and started to rummage through its pockets. At first, he couldn't find it. The inside pocket, why is my phone here, he thought. The spider web cracked screen was getting worse, Spruyt couldn't read the number or name of the caller. He answered anyway.

    'Deano's bail-bonding service; you fail'em, we bail'em.'

    'Hi.'

    Cachi.

    It was Beth. Panic rattled his already fragile bones. What has he done now? Spruyt could only guess. All scenarios were nightmare based, veiled in a curtain of

Afterbirth

unpleasantness. Spruyt wasn't normally a drunk dialer, he tended to avoid his phone after he was two or more ales in, to avoid this exact situation. He was on his first solo flight here, without any training or co-pilot. Spruyt was very close to just hanging up outright.

'Hey you, everything okay?'

Beth laughed, a little relief washed over Spruyt as it sounded genuine. It's not all lost then, he pondered. She replied, 'All dandy here, how's everything with Paul Smith? Apart from the sales, I mean.'

Spruyt said through a cough, 'Jigger please, it's all good here at casa Smith.'

'*Really?* I've seen news reports of a wild man fitting your description running around and upsetting people. Like a pocket-sized Putin.' Okay, Spruyt thought, maybe everything is lost.

'Well, I don't want to accuse you of being misinformed, but all reports from here show the western front saw no action last night. You need to check your sources, Elizabeth.'

'Okay,' she said rather abruptly. Spruyt wanted to slap himself, he'd pushed her too far. Silence rang down the line for several moments. Had she hung up? Spruyt couldn't tell. The hangover slapped him around the head a few more times for good measure. Then, like a foghorn through the mist, 'Hi Paulie, it's Beth here. I need to check the validation of your report, I'm being accused of lying?' Spruyt could hear the smile in her voice. He let out a few quiet chuckles whilst thinking, what on earth did I do?

'Listen, sorry if any calls or texts came through sounding odd. I'd like to blame it on the ale but that's not strictly true, I tend to be a bit wonky even without the stuff.'

'Well, I'd like to see that, I've only witnessed the ale fueled madness,' her reply was warm like a summer's day. Heating up Spruyt's cold-but-somehow-sweat-soaked skin. She went on, 'Not the most usual reply, true, but I enjoyed it. It was very original.'

Spruyt weighed up his options; he was a mess, that was clear. He'd known that for some time. Beth, she deserves better. As did Marie before he nuked that whole relationship too. Even Thom, the poor guy was only trying to help and he'd ripped the piss out of him for no other reason than it was his default setting. I've lost Marie already, Spruyt told himself, and I'll lose the others if I'm not careful. This circus needs to be turned around to head in the right direction before it's too late. Also, Spruyt knew, he had nothing else to lose, so ask.

'Well, I can arrange that for you, if you are prepared for it.'

'Yeah, sure you can,' she replied.

'I'm serious,' Spruyt said, a little hurt (and somewhat surprised he was), 'I'd like to take you out sometime. Proper likes. No glasses, just plates and cutlery and un-slurred words. Maybe some low lightening, a hipster style waiter with the tash with gel in it, all twisted up at points at the end, you know, the full works.' Spruyt held his breath, he could feel his face turning Liverpool red.

'I'd like that,' that smile in her voice echoing down the line again. Spruyt wanted to reach into the phone and hug her. After this, they set a time and date. Hanging up, Spruyt screamed the house down. It was a positive release of energy but looking on you wouldn't have thought so. He did it several times, knowing that since the house next door and across the street were vacant, no alarms would be raised.

With a newfound & sea deep love for life, Spruyt peeled himself off the sofa and headed to the kitchen. He started to make some coffee. While he waited for it to percolate, he went through his messages. Sure as death and taxes, Beth's message had been replied too. The timestamp was from an unholy hour of the morning. This was the only thing Spruyt could see, the rest read *message deleted*. Spruyt couldn't believe it; he must have replied to Beth's message and even in his ale-riddled brain decided it was too embarrassing to keep record of. So, using unquestionable ale logic, he'd deleted the message because that solves everything. Pouring out his coffee, he swore at himself.

The hangover was trying its best to keep its assault upon Spruyt's body but it was failing. Some sort of shield was up making its attempts at the achy muscles and headache and sicken guts damper than usual, weaker. Something was changing.

He opened the back door to the kitchen and saw the grey skies and the light rain. A mist, almost hovering in the air, it looked more like snow than rain. He saw this but didn't feel it. He sat down on the step, coffee in hand, and watched what was left of the morning tick away.

His new lust for life was leaving him. He knew why but he tried not to think about it. He failed. Sipping his ever-cooling coffee, Spruyt had already registered the shine of what had caused the tide of his mood to turn.

    The BBQ was still there in the yard. It'd never been used for its proper purposes. Like so much in Spruyt's house, it had been brought with such grand intentions and then left to collect dust. Sipping away, he wondered why so much dust collected in and around his house. It was a one-person household, is that all from me alone?

    Honestly, the man just can't focus.

    The house had been left in Spruyt's name by his Nan. This surprised him as Marie and his Nan had always gotten on so well. He'd assumed it would be left to both of them.

™© *Z M Barrett*

Still, it was an astute move from the old lady in a way. Almost like she knew what was coming.

Spruyt and Marie had been in the house several weeks from what he could remember. They'd possessed the house for almost a year but so much work was required before they could move in. The kitchen and bathroom had been done but living between this house and their old flat was too much of a financial burden. So, they moved in. With all the focus on the inside of the house, getting that up to snuff, the deed issue had fallen behind. Marie trusted him, there was no reason not too. On arrival into the house on that first night, she tasked him with transferring the deed from his name into both their names. Spruyt agreed without any real zeal or passion. Marie just thought it was him being him, the daydreamer. Partly, that was true. But there was more.

Spruyt didn't want to do it. Had the choice been taken from him by his Nan, like he'd assumed it would have been, he'd not have had a problem with it. But now with the choice left to him, Spruyt knew what he was

Afterbirth

going to choose. He knew too, within himself, that he wouldn't change the deed as Marie had asked him to.

If this wasn't scary enough, the real kicker was the fact he had *no* reason to feel this way. Sure, they'd had a few fights before moving into the house but nothing more. This was way back before all the *real* bad stuff had started. I can't do it, he'd often find himself thinking during the day at work or when trying to sleep at night. The worry was all-consuming. I can't do it, Spruyt was always thinking, and I don't know why.

It isn't anger, disappointment or violence, that ends a relationship. It's the indifferent stagnation, the lack of anything other than a chosen void, an allowed silence you both let fall & fester between you, that kills you dead.

That ends everything.

Marie pestered him on this as the weeks went by. All she knew was he was dragging his feet, being the airhead he was. Spruyt left this as long as he could until a shouting match began over it. He had no choice, the paperwork was soon drawn up. When the papers arrived from the lawyers, Marie went through each line with a fine-tooth comb. Spruyt left her to it, it didn't matter what was in that writing. No matter what way it was worded, once it was signed-off and handed back, it was game over.

He was in the kitchen, zoned out into his cold coffee. Marie came in chatting about something or another, all Spruyt heard was static. He was just feeling a foreboding within his chest. It was a civil war within, one side rallying behind Marie and the life they were trying to build together, the other standing firm and holding them back, screaming death before anything else. Spruyt had no idea which side he wanted to win; he couldn't even understand why the war had started.

'Are you even listening to me?'

'Hmm?'

Marie stood there, her hand holding out a large vanilla envelope towards him. Her other hand was resting on her hip which was at an angle.

'So rude, jump out of your head and listen! I need to see Val after I've stopped off at work, so can you drop this off at Austin's please?' Spruyt nodded as she waited for him to take the large envelope off her. He couldn't. Spruyt knew once he had that paperwork, he'd do something stupid. Accepting he wouldn't take it, Marie shook her head and placed it gently on the table. Picking up her handbag from the empty seat in the process, she bid goodbye to Spruyt. She found it strange when he silently stood up and saw her out. He walked like a man being led to the gallows. She sensed a heaviness in Spruyt she could only feel and not ask about. He kissed her goodbye and shut the door as she left.

    He stood there for some time. Then, his body moved. Spruyt only saw this, he didn't feel it. He'd left it and was following from behind it in the third-person. Looking over his own shoulder, Spruyt watched his body slowly walk back into the kitchen. What's it going to do, he pondered. His body slowly walked past the table and without looking picked up the vanilla envelope containing the newly signed deed. Tucking this under its arm, he watched as it went to a draw and took out a box of matches whilst grabbing the all-purpose rum off the kitchen top. Still watching on, Spruyt couldn't understand what his body was doing.

    Walking outside, Spruyt's body lifted the BBQ lid and placed the new deed inside. With that on the never-used grill, it poured some of the rum onto it. Still peaking over his shoulder in the third-person as it tried to light a match, Spruyt couldn't work out what this was. The first match broke because his body struck it so violently. The second one took, its scratch of life bouncing off the yard walls. The new deed went up in a burst of flames. All Spruyt saw from his point-of-view was the flames crawling across the envelope like water soaking through a sponge. The heat burned his face. Spruyt only rejoined his body after the last of the ashes dropped through the grill.

Presently, Spruyt downs the last of his coffee dregs and moves over to the BBQ. Opening it and going full De Niro again, he looked into the ashes. They were still there. Lingering in the abyss, controlling way more than they should. Spruyt couldn't decide whether he was weak for allowing it to do this or not. He took out his phone and tried to find the number. The cracked screen held him up something fierce. Eventually, he found the one he was looking for. He called it.

'Hullo?' The voice was shaky, unsure. This was a call from the past it was never expecting.

'Arthur Whistle's post-boxing therapy group; you floor'em, we cure'em.'

She took a big inhale of breath, Spruyt could see her clasping her temples in frustration already. 'What do you want, Paul?'

'Marie, hi.'

Spruyt hung up and felt drained. It was more than just the hangover which was still sitting heavy on his shoulders. Emotionally, he'd been drained and rinsed out like a cheap water-soaked tissue. It was nothing more than arranging a meeting with Marie. He was standing at the foot of the mountain and already he was suffering from altitude sickness.

™© *Z M Barrett*

Coming back in from the yard, Spruyt locked the door and left his used mug in the sink. He climbed the questioning stairs at a pace similar to the OJ Simpson car chase. Laboriously slow, with the occasional threat of danger. Impaired motor skills from the hangover combined with the steep and narrow staircase almost bested Spruyt. It aged him, truly. On the victory of reaching the top, he stripped off his clothes and entered the bathroom. He kept his eyes down so he didn't catch the excusing reflection's gaze; he couldn't face that today. On setting the toothpaste on his brush, he closed his eyes whilst cleaning his teeth. It was a token gesture and he worked them poorly.

After this, he switched the shower on and grabbed his clippers. He stubbed his toe on the corner of the bath as he forgot to open his eyes and cursed aloud. He shaved down the past few days stubble whilst standing in the warm water of the shower. Spruyt felt calm but empty. He turned the water temperature up until it was just below burning on his skin. He then sat down and stretched out underneath the water. He'd

Afterbirth

been here before, so he knew the water had to be warmer on immediate release from the showerhead as it would be colder by the time it hit him whilst he was lying down. Resting his left forearm across his forehead, he closed his eyes again and tried to block out everything. As he fell into a doze, the only thing he could hear was the falling of the water.

Sometime later, Spruyt woke with a shudder. The water was still going but was as cold as an early morning rain in November. Sitting up but not standing, he turned off the water. Hunched over his knees, he clasped his hands together and sat there for several more moments. He could feel his skin crawling with the cold. The hangover had jumped off his shoulders now but it was still beating him in the stomach and lower intestine. He waited it out. His insides turned violently, causing sweat and nausea to break throughout his body. It felt like someone had reached inside of him, grabbed his guts and stomach, and were pulling them apart at all horrible angles, tying them around each other. It came in waves, receding slowly and then coming back in full force. Spruyt waited for a low break before he got up, as quickly as he could in his state, and towelled off. He got into bed just as a new wave started. He doubled-over and swore at all of god's creation for the pain he was enduring. An uneasy sleep came but only in fits and starts. Spruyt was just under the surface of his consciousness feeling the pain raging inside him.

  The light faded, night came, the pain was there throughout.

He decided to get up sometime around noon. Feeling weak, paper-thin, Spruyt burned some toast then binned it. The second attempt came out much better but even with hot butter dripping off the slices that were lightly toasted a golden brown, he had no desire to eat them. After three cups of coffee, he managed to force one slice down. Using a system of three sips bite, three sips bite, he managed to trick his gut into thinking he was just drinking not eating. I'm in a Mexican stand-off with my own body, Spruyt thought.

He made another call, this time to Thom. He put the feelers out for a meeting in a few weeks time. It felt nice to be putting things in motion. To be readying that saddle for a ride. This is a commitment though, he told himself, you have to follow it through. See Marie and ace the interview with Thom. Things need closure and you need resolve. Spruyt's pep-talk to himself left him feeling weaker. Unable to climb the stairs, he retreated to the front room. Picking up the discarded jacket that was still on the floor, he covered himself and tried to sleep. It wasn't a full reset or release of normal sleep. More like a diet sleep, a sleep lite. When he did dream, he was surrounded by flames. A wreckage of his own making.

A few more days passed like this. Spruyt, not trusting himself on the outside of the walls he lived, boxed himself in. He lived off council pop and all the tinned/frozen goods that remained in the house. He was using a hundred-and-fifty pound kettle to make pot noodles, a two-grand oven to heat-up everyday value sausages rolls and piercing the film lids of his still-life ready meals with knife blades worth more than the clothes he was wearing.

He'd spent part of the night fetal on the front room floor, riding out waves of pain again. Shivering in the moonlight, Spruyt could feel his rancid sweat pool under his arms and sit in his crouch. Even his hangover looked on, impressed with the effect of this new condition, bringing Spruyt to the brink. It watched on hoping to pick up tips for new techniques it could use. Game recognise game.

The damp smell of wet dog filled his nose, his vision became blurred in both tears and thick bullets of sweat.

A few times he thought he'd be out-willed by his sickness and shat himself. Spruyt didn't, thank god, but he came mighty close.

'Do you want a drink?'
No response. Buried into her chair, Marie looked on at whatever was on the screen. Spruyt had been buried in his work laptop staring at pictures of wallpaper

designs for hours. This was for the bedroom and he'd be more excited about getting his appendix removed without anaesthetic. Spruyt was going to the kitchen, he just asked her for something to say. To break the tension. It'd be building for some time and he had no idea why. He repeated his question.

Marie didn't answer, she just looked over at Spruyt. She looked thoughtful, sincere. She swung back to the screen and saw they'd been a break in play or an advert come up or such. She stood up whilst saying, 'No thanks.' She left the room and Spruyt heard her climb the narrow stairs and close the bathroom door. He knew it was the bathroom because of the sound of it. The action of the door closing echoed off the titles, bounced down the stairs and landed in the hallway.

Spruyt stared at the wall but did not see it. This was a week or two after their last altercation that had left his nose in its current wonky state. He shook his head in a vain attempt to come back to himself. It didn't work. Maybe she knew about the deed, he pondered. He closed his laptop and decided to take a walk. Sitting in this tension was suffocating. Standing, he noticed Marie's phone. She'd never leave her phone when using the facilities. She was a diehard squat-n-surfer. Watching himself from the third-person again, he picked up the phone and punched her code in. They knew each other's codes in a daring game of trust. Whether Marie recalled this or not, no one knows.

Opening straight away to her messages, he saw a picture of himself. Sat at the kitchen table, a vacant glaze of shock in his eyes, hands flat on the table. His nose gushing with blood. No words were written underneath. Spruyt didn't even look at who it'd been sent too; it didn't matter. All he knew, from that exact point, is that she'd had reduced him to nothing. He was a no-man. He was a joke and now other people, people in the *real* world knew it. There was no pride left, no masculinity left, just pity.

Locking the phone, Spruyt's mouth twisted into a dark shade of evil. It wasn't a plan as such, just a feeling of what had to be done. That money that'd been banked, well, it was now time to be withdrawn.

She sat there, toilet lid down, hands underneath her chin, and wanted to cry. The river had run dry, though. That river of emotion, that waterfall of her spirit was nothing more than a tiny puddle surrounded by an encroaching desert. There was no need to send that message, to remonstrate the issues they were having to outside parties. It can't be that bad, they'd all protest. Oh yeah? select picture, send. Thank you & goodnight.

    He'd done something stupid again, something air-headed. For the life of her, Marie couldn't even recall what it was. Now, people knew what *she* was. A creature capable of terrible things. Reduced to using fists and no words to express herself. Part of her soul had cracked every time she let herself drop into that mode of destruction. Spruyt would've never said anything, he was trapped in the bully complex. Marie knew this and it made her feel even worse. She couldn't go back in that room, the tension floated around them like a steam room. She heard Spruyt step into the hallway and stop. She looked up at the closed door. Something felt off, wonky. The pressure of the silence was so big she thought her eardrums were going to implode. That her brain would leak out the blown-out wounds. At some point, Marie heard the muffled shutting of the front door.

Opening the bathroom door, she looked down the narrow staircase and tried to understand the feeling that was left in the house. Marie could feel no more tension but it wasn't empty either. She could still feel the electricity of something in the atmosphere. Something still lurked there, something unknown.

Spruyt went to the shop on the corner. He brought his first-ever bottle of vodka, no bag. It swished back and forwards in his hand like clear deceit. It looked like water. He stared at it intently as he walked back towards the house.

Marie needed to talk to someone. Help her understand her own motives and what she was trying to do to Spruyt, to herself. Picking up her coat and bag, she left the house in search of help.

Afterbirth

He saw her leave from across the road. Hood up, sat on the step of the vacant house across from them, Marie paid him no mind. He followed her stride to the car. She started up and left. He waited ten minutes more before he went in. To be sure.

She parked up outside the house some hours later. Marie knew something was wrong already. The pressure was off, the air around her didn't sit right. Marie wanted to get back in the car and drive off. No answers came, no pathways of solutions. But now, it might be too late.

    The first step into the house revealed the crunch of glass. It was eerie silent, like the gaps between thunder. She followed the trail which led into the front room.

    The TV was no more. It sat face down on the middle of the floor. The screen glass was everywhere. The plastic casing of the thing had been obliterated. It looked like it'd been thrown into a wood chipper. Her face looked like that scream painting, mouth agape to a horrible hole, no teeth showing and eyes as wide as plates. It was as silent as the painting too. Marie made no sound other than her landing into the lawn of glass beneath her. It cut and embedded itself into both her knee caps. Thick blood like spilt wine poured out of her cuts into the carpet.

Spruyt saw all this from his propped up position next to the fireplace. The wrench was by his right hand, the bottle of poison in his left. He looked ridiculous crammed into that tutu. He'd ripped it heavily at the shoulders and waist. Along with his recently crooked nose, his face was covered in tiny scratches from the screen of the TV as he battered it to death. He'd caught a few, for sure. Not all of them, but some of them left scars. Tiny little ones that you couldn't see but could feel.

He looked on and waited. The first few minutes passed like the lowering of a coffin into the ground. Then, the wailing started. The weeping and face of a crushed soul, surrounded by blood and glass looked at him, and wailed out a pain that sounded like the gate to hell opening. He felt himself lose all

Afterbirth

vigour and purpose for what he had already committed.

That bitch, Spruyt thought, my one victory and she can't even let me have that.

Soon after Spruyt's complete loss of control, the issue of the deed was made known. He couldn't remember how it came to light, but Spruyt wouldn't have put it past him to implicate himself. He was the kamikaze pilot that had flown straight into their relationship. Nothing was left now, just memories. Good & bad, they were all poisoned with the horridness of how it ended.

After Marie left, that deep kind of obsidian silence fell over the house. A suffocating silence, like the ones you get after a single distant gunshot.

Presently, he was sat up by the fireplace again. The waves of pain were still there but his memories were just as vicious. Spruyt was poisoned in the head and body now. He had no idea how this was going to play out. All he knew was that he was going to have to play. Try, at least. His effort was draining already.

™© *Z M Barrett*

Marie was already at their table when he entered the place. He felt exposed, marked. Despite seeing her at the table, he went to the person on the door to go through the motions. She'd be staring into her phone screen but it was her alright. The hair had been chopped down in a pixie style and dyed a bright blonde from dark brown. The thick-stencilled eyebrows were still in play (she had a thing about them, they were too fair in her option so were always filled in) but her skin was far darker than normal. A holiday or self-tan? Spruyt couldn't tell. Her hands were littered with rings, that was new. When he arrived at the table she looked up and smiled with only her mouth. The eyes were stern in their gaze, distant. The faux smile did highlight her cheekbones, Spruyt had always loved those cheekbones.

She'd put her phone away. It was the same one from all those nights ago, Spruyt noted. He then began to wonder why he'd even bothered to think that. Like it mattered in some way. Marie was waiting for him to

Afterbirth

speak. He was waiting for the same. It was awkward.

A waiter came and asked for a drinks order. Marie asked for a G&T, Spruyt for a cranberry juice. That did it.

'Cranberry juice?'

'I know of it, yes.' Here we go, Spruyt thought. We're picking up where we left off. Falling into old dynamics or like a book you didn't finish and had no intention of picking up again. Vacant words said for the sake of them. He closed his eyes and moved his head from left to right. You knew what you'd signed up for, some inner voice spat at him.

Marie said, 'Are you trying to impress me or something?'

'Well, clearly it is working.'

Cue silence.

Neither of them could understand it. As the hum of the restaurant around them filled their connectionless void, Marie started to ponder why she'd got at Spruyt. There was no reason for it, she thought. If he is trying to get off the ale, then great. Good for him. Why am I treating that as a sign of weakness? Marie couldn't work it out and this scared her.

™© *Z M Barrett*

Like most people who have fallen out of love and put each other through ringers and ringers of emotional hell, they were in a constant state of sparring. Looking for an opening even when the bell had gone and the round had ended.

Spruyt could feel the sweat beading on his forehead. Another wave was on its way. A spasm hit him hard, which caused Spruyt to lean forward. Marie pulled back slightly, trying to work out what Spruyt was up too. He tried to cover it by crossing his arms and planting them on the table. Like it was always planned. Marie knew it wasn't. She watched him from her new vantage point and watched the colour drain from his face. Marie saw the paleness crawl over him like a shadow.

'Are you okay?'

Spruyt knew this question was coming. He felt the cold creep through his face, then his arms and legs. He knew this was the colour leaving him. Amongst the pain in his guts was the panic of it happening. Right here, in a *public* place.

'Paul?'

Marie was right there, across from him at the table. This wasn't how it sounded to Spruyt, though. Her words seemed muffled like she was speaking from behind a wall or underwater or something. Another wave caused Spruyt to crumble his face in agony. Cold sweat was pouring off his head like rain.

'I'll be right back,' Spruyt tried to say. It came out more in groans than words. He only got a few steps away...

...the sky was blue. An electric blue, crystalline with not a cloud in sight. Spruyt was calmly walking through a vast hayfield. Surrounded by the warm gold harvest, Spruyt didn't have a single coherent thought in his head. He lifted his hands up so he could feel the tops of the crop field surrounding him. As far as he could see, it was all still gold and blue. There was no breeze. He could feel the heat of the sun on his skin and the waving of his wake behind him as he walked. His pace was slow...

Spruyt wasn't aware of opening his eyes. The images of table legs, people's feet and the

™© *Z M Barrett*

floor just faded into his vision. There was a small amount of blood in front of him. He was lying on his side on the floor so he tried to get up but couldn't. As soon as he tried to sit up, he was pushed back down. Spruyt slowly became aware of someone holding his head. He couldn't speak.

'He's awake,' he heard Marie say. Her words were soaked with tears.

'Paulie, can you hear me?'

Spruyt said nothing, he just tried to nod. 'Don't move your head or fall asleep, Paulie. You need to stay awake now.'

When Spruyt lost consciousness, he came down on the back of his head. His full weight. It split open like a watermelon. Marie screamed and ran over to his prone body. An off-duty nurse, who was having his own meal three tables away, soon followed her. He rolled Spruyt onto his side and kept his head straight. Blood covered his hands and soaked through Spruyt's hair. Marie was shook but she managed to tell the nurse his name. Holding paper towels and cloths to Spruyt's head to try and stem the bleeding, the nurse said, 'Stay awake now Paulie, don't fall back asleep.'

    That was me. I said that.

I hope I haven't shat meself, Spruyt thought, after being awake for a few moments on the floor. That really would be an insult to injury. He hadn't. The crushing pain inside of his guts had dissipated too. Gone, like smoke on the water. He desperately wanted to get up and leave. Walk out the door and leave this sorry mess behind him. They wouldn't let him, though. He could hear panicked voices asking for towels or ambulances or help from operators. Lying there, he started to feel the back of his head swell. He still couldn't talk. Spruyt wasn't sure if this was because he couldn't or he didn't want to.

    'The ambulance is on its way,' I was told. Surprising, I remember thinking, as Spruyt was an adult and the cut wasn't the largest (but bleeding profusely), it would have been a low priority, barely touching the category scale the response centre use. I told Spruyt this and got no response.

It was like stepping inside a fluorescent light, the inners of the ambulance. Spruyt was lying there on the bed, wondering if anyone had died whilst lying in this spot. It felt strangely impersonal, clinical. One of the paramedics was sitting in the back with Spruyt speaking to Marie. Chatting about something. Spruyt heard none of it, he barely even saw it.

Spruyt was wheeled into the hospital doors like an invalid. Pushed into the waiting room, he was left at the end of a row of seats. Marie sat in the empty chair next to him, her head down with her gaze locked onto her scrolling. She was trying and failing to distract herself from Spruyt's sudden glimpse of mortality. He just sat there with dry blood on his head and shoulder, trying to place this event somewhere in his life's tapestry. Was it to be a big side of it or just a small square in the corner? Be in the middle or at the end?
    Spruyt wasn't sure.

Marie sat with him in the ward for some time. She spoke at him rather than to him. Inbetween Marie's sentences, the noise of the

Afterbirth

ward never stopped. Screams of pain came from other beds, the nonsensical pleading of patients clearly no longer on the same planet. It made Spruyt feel so much worse. Once he found his voice again, he tried to send Marie home but she refused until he'd been seen by a doctor. Spruyt was still thinking about that tapestry.

The incessant beeping of the monitor was driving Spruyt crazy. Every time he looked over his BPM was always in three figures. His heart was rattling his chest again, he could see it through his torso smacking the inside of his ribcage.

    The wound in his head wasn't deep enough for stitches so the doctor had glued it closed. Spruyt could feel stray drops of it drying in his hair around the cut. The doctor had also told him the options for his erratic heartbeat; they could either put him on a drip to bring his heart back down to a normal rate or put him to sleep and shock him awake to reset the rhythm. Marie turned away from Spruyt when she heard this. When she brought her face back her eyes were clingfilmed in tears. Spruyt thought about being put to sleep, like a sick dog, never to wake again. Had his options really reduced that much?

Spruyt didn't sleep, he just tried to vacate himself. He was trying to get back to that hayfield. All that gold and blue, peaceful in its wake. He failed.

When the doctor did return with his decision, he tried the monitor one last time. Spruyt was now down to two figures, what a lucky guy you are, the doctor said. Spruyt asked if he could still have the shock anyway, he didn't laugh. As he left, Spruyt turned to Marie and asked her to leave again. She didn't want to but there was nothing more she could do. He asked her to come back in the morning to take him home. She agreed. Marie walked off the ward with her head down and her soul drained. When he was alone, Spruyt tried to cry. It felt like it was necessary. The tears didn't come.

Afterbirth

Spruyt changed back into his clothes and was led off the ward. He felt better being dressed in his own clothes but the nurses still wouldn't let him walk. He was wheeled to the lift and taken up several floors. He didn't make note of which floor was their destination.

Finding himself in another waiting room, he brought his hand up to the back of his head. A shot of pain went through the back of his eyes as the tip of his finger touched a hair close to the wound.

Another nurse collected him and took him into a small consultation room. He was given a pocket monitor which looked like a pager from the nineties. Three long cables grew from this which held the pads that were to be stuck to his chest. Colour coded, the yellow one was attached to his left side, the green to just under his neck in the centre of his chest and the red one to the right side. His heart was to be monitored for the next five days or so. He'd suffered an episode of atrial fibrillation, or AF as they kept calling it. They told Spruyt it was probably due to the drop in blood pressure caused by the abdominal pain.

Still, they had to be sure. Spruyt was given a folder with extra pads in and a booklet to write down any symptoms or issues that occurred during the next few days. He was to bring it back after a few days and return it to the front desk. The nurse asked him to sign for the monitor.

'It just to say you'll bring it back,' the nurse said while pointing at where to sign, 'not that you'll sell it on eBay or something.'

'You got me.'

Spruyt was discharged earlier than he planned. He was going to call Marie and ask her to pick him up but then he decided against it. After he was fitted with his portable monitor, he was allowed to walk again. His legs felt like stilts, ungainly and hard to walk on. He walked out of the hospital slowly, like the pace he had in the hayfield. Outside, the sky was grey and on the cusp of rainfall. Seeing a park to his immediate left, Spruyt headed towards it. He found a vacant bench and sat down. Taking out the monitor, he looked at it with disgust. It felt like he was holding a timebomb, it could go off at any

Afterbirth

minute. No, Spruyt thought, if my days are numbered, I don't want to know by how many. He ripped off the pads and placed it back in the folder. Spruyt returned it to the hospital as instructed. He exited again and tried to call Marie. His hands wouldn't let him.

He couldn't put his finger on it, what he felt like. Sitting back at the park, Spruyt was struggling to put his thoughts in order. He felt something about his situation, he just couldn't conceptualise it within his thinking. He slapped himself hard, trying to kick his brain into gear. Swing and a miss. Closing his eyes, Spruyt prayed no one saw what he'd just done.

    It drifted up into his thought palace some time afterwards. Still sitting there, not feeling the heavy breeze or rain on his body, he saw what it was in the smoke of his mind. He felt like his own afterbirth. That was it; his old life had been borne into a new one and he was the muck that followed it. All the gory placenta and fetal membranes that spattered on the frictionless-white floor. He was what followed the joy of new life, the waste, the unwanted by-product. And if he wasn't careful, he was going to get swept away and sent to the medical dump.

Finally, his hands managed to dial Marie.
'Hullo?'
'Mama & Papa's blue-collar non-nonsense nursery; you bore'em, we adore'em.'
She laughed before she responded, it was full of more life than Spruyt had ever felt, 'Need that lift then?'

Marie dropped Spruyt off outside his front door. He walked up to it and placed the key inside. He turned back to the road to wave her off as she pulled away. Standing there, Spruyt watched her drive to the end of the road and turn. Once she was out of sight, he withdrew his key and walked away from the house. Slowly, tortoise slow, he walked to the shop. There was only one thing on his mind.
'Do you need a bag?'
'Does the Vatican help police prosecute its paedophile members?'

Afterbirth

Spruyt exited the shop with the clear bottle of liquid clasped in his hand. It's clear contents bobbled up and down as he walked. The clamminess of his hand rocketed up. At one point, Spruyt pondered if the bottle was leaking, there was that much moisture. Stopping outside his house, he lifted the bottle up to be the main focus of his vision. Tell me, Spruyt thought, tell me what you want. Silence, nothing.

That was just it; it wanted nothing.

Spruyt stood there for several more moments on this thought. Then, he pulled his hand back and threw the vodka at the house on the opposite side of the street. Smashing on the top step, the elixir of deceit splashed onto the bottom of the door and all over the three steps. He felt a breeze picking up. He turned away from the street and entered his house.

Spruyt spent the next few days pottering about his house. He'd also suffered a concussion from his fall, so he still felt ropey in the head. Well, more than usual. There was no further passing-out or vomiting which the

™© *Z M Barrett*

hospital warned him about, though. (He was to return to them if one or both of these things occurred.) At first, it felt like someone was kicking his head from the inside. He'd go about his business in the house trying not to think of such words as banging, explosion, hammering, pulsating. Tried not to picture his brain ripping from its lining in his skull. Don't think collision, seize or brain damage, Spruyt'd tell himself. Four days later or so the pain had all but subsided in his lump of lead. Sometimes though, at night, he would wake up thinking he was still wearing that portable monitor.

    He spoke to both Thom & Beth, going out of his way *not* to mention his brush with weakness. With mortality. He was grateful to Marie for staying with him and getting him home. He couldn't speak to her, though. Whether it was due to embarrassment or fear of what happened could happen again, he wasn't so sure.

Can someone see their future? Spruyt was constantly thinking about this as he pottered around his house during these long & lonely days after the hospital.

Eventually, he decided no, they can't. After all that internal debate, all that back and forth with his own subconscious, this was Spruyt's final decision on the matter. No, they can't see their own future, but he did decide they could *feel* it. He knew this from his own recent experience, of all that foreboding, of that feeling of something bigger than himself happening. Despite trying to live in that void, fate had come hunting him out anyway. The more he thought about this, the more he realised Marie had felt the same about her own life, her own journey. The future wasn't images or pictures, it was a feeling. It was an instinct.

The lock of the front door sounded off. Spruyt was sitting at the kitchen table with a cup of coffee that had long gone cold. There was only one other person who had a key to the house. He let out a small, laboured cough.

Marie appeared at the kitchen door. 'After everything that happened with us,' she folded her arms as she walked into the kitchen, 'and you still didn't bother getting the locks changed?' Spruyt laughed a little. He went to take a sip of his drink. As soon as the ice-cold liquid hit his lips he spat it back into the mug. 'I was waiting for you to sort it for me. Like I'd do something for myself.' Marie smiled. She pulled out a chair to join Spruyt when he offered her a drink. Leaving the chair pulled away from the table, Marie grabbed Spruyt's mug and walked over the sink. She switched the kettle on and fished out a mug of her own like she owned the place. It took Spruyt a few seconds to remember that she should have owned the place, in all fairness.

She couldn't help herself, 'God! I love this kitchen.'

'It loves you.'

'Shame you didn't,' there was a little humour in her voice but it papered over some very bitter feelings.

'Yeah, well,' Spruyt spat out, 'I'm a child of divorce.'

Marie let a sly smile creep onto her face as she shook her head at his reply. They both knew Spruyt had never even met his parents, let alone knew if they had gotten divorced or

Afterbirth

even married in the first place. Marie wanted to get angry at this, at him deflecting her comment with a silly joke, but she held her tongue. If they fell out now, this past mess between them would never get resolved. Briefly, she thought she could feel blood on her teeth from biting down on her words so aggressively.

    She returned to the table, placing Spruyt's fresh mug of coffee down. She placed her own mug down, it was the 'UNT' one. 'Rules are rules,' she said. Spruyt raised his own mug in a cheers gesture, Marie mimicked this and they sipped quietly together.

    'How's the head?'

    'Mental.'

    'I meant physically,' Marie replied.

    'Bumpy. I can't get the glue out of my hair, it looks like some bloke has spaffed his beans into it.' As she laughed he turned his head around to show her. It didn't look that bad but it had clumped in several places around the cut. It had dried in a colour of an aged yellow, like a smoker's fingernails.

™© *Z M Barrett*

'So, are you going to start or am I?'

Spruyt couldn't decide which would be worse. There were things they both needed to sort, to clear the stagnant air between them. Eventually, he replied, 'Ladies first.'

'Dickhead.'

Marie wrapped both her hands around the warm mug of joe. She knew this had to happen but the words simply won't come. Staring into the dark warm liquid, Marie just let her voice start, hoping the words would follow. Voice shaking, she heard herself speak, not feel it. She talked about the person she'd become because of him, the way he treated her and himself. How she knew that it wasn't just that, she was responsible too for letting herself slip into that kind of person.

'And for that, I am sorry.'

Spruyt let out a small chuckle before smiling and dropping his head down. His voice laced with strain, he asked 'what do you want from this? *Need* from this? Because I know I need something, I just can't put it into words.'

Marie thought about this for a few moments. She released the mug from her hands and leaned forward onto the table with crossed arms. 'I'm the same, I think. The future is there, waiting, but I'm just hanging back, loitering in a present I never thought I would have. Not being with you, I mean.'

Spruyt continued to keep his head down as Marie went on.

'As bad as it got, as horrible as we treated each other, no part of me believed it would end. So now, I have to re-align the stars, find a new north.' Spruyt wiped his eyes with the back of his hand before lifting his head.

'For me, it's living *with* the past. Whenever I try to move on, it comes back at me and knocks me down. I think about how I treated you, the things I let slip, the things I never said about how I felt and the things I did say or how I acted just to hurt you. Sure, you lashed out a few times. Left some marks. I was no better, though. The marks I left on you are psychological, but they are still scars.'

Marie took one of her hands out and put it on Spruyt's. She squeezed it. Spruyt returned this pressure. He whispered an almost inaudible apology. She reciprocated

™© *Z M Barrett*

but was somehow even quieter than him, which caused Marie to laugh as more tears started to flow.

Spruyt said, 'Our future is uncertain, as is the past.'

'What?'

'Our past is uncertain. It keeps coming into the present, breaking its form from linear to non-linear. I can see it is haunting you. It's trying to insert itself into my future too. Can you see it? It's taunting both of us on what we used to have and how bad we can be as a person to someone else. Someone we used to love. The taunting is masking its destruction of the present, of the future. Removing it one brick at a time until there is nothing left but a hollow foundation. An all-encompassing void. I can't let that happen. *We* can't let that happen to each other.'

'We won't,' Marie said.

Spruyt saw Marie out. They hugged before she left. It was a warm embrace. When the door closed, he felt the energy drain from his body. It ran off him like a waterfall. Exhausted, he climbed the narrow staircase. Removing his trainers and all other clothes apart from his boxers, he climbed into bed.

The dead don't sleep this well.

A few days later, Spruyt was greeted by a Darth Vader made of PEE. He'd opened his front door to let the sunshine in. Mid-morning, it had already been unusually warm. The old homestead was heating up, fast, so Spruyt wanted to let in some fresh air. Also, the extra light from the sun would make the place look a little brighter, he thought.

And there she was.

Spruyt could only tell it was a she by her height & the few wisps of light blonde/grey hair that were on show. The masks covered every other feature. Yes, *masks*. Along with the cloth face mask over her mouth & nose, and the safety goggles on her eyes, she was also wearing one of those clear sneeze-guard masks over all that. A disposable plastic apron wrinkled like an old carrier bag & white skin-tight latex gloves completed this look.

Stupefied, Spruyt looked on. He momentarily thought about the portable

™© *Z M Barrett*

monitor, maybe they knew he'd crapped out. Maybe they were expecting him to be dead on the floor of his fancy kitchen or something. PEE Vader also remained silent for several moments.

Her hands held nothing, but to her right on the floor was a heavy bag, full of tubes, air canisters, bandages, the unmistakable green/white plus-sign of a first-aid kit.

'Did you call an ambulance?'

'No,' Spruyt coughed out, the words & action both small & laboured in nature.

'Is this number thirteen?' Her words were muffled too, due to all the safety precautions she was wearing. Speaking through a gag of her own making, for fear of what was outside it.

'It is, but which street did you want?' PEE Vader told him, she was at the right number but the wrong street. I know that feeling, he thought. Spruyt stepped out into the sun and directed her to where she needed to go.

I'm the hero of a story no one ever told, Spruyt thought.

Afterbirth

Sometime later, Spruyt couldn't help but find himself wondering if PEE Vader had reached her destination. Several times, in fact, he got up to leave and walk around to the street she wanted several hours before. To check, to make sure all was well. And several times, he'd yell at himself internally.

    What's the point, his mind screamed, you're too late.

The waves of pain still came but their current was much weaker than they had been. The change in diet seemed to be working. Reduced coffee intake, no more cheese, no more drinking. Spruyt hadn't realised how hollow he'd felt in his body in recent months. It was amazing, he thought, for such change after only a few weeks. He was also managing to keep the house clean. One afternoon, he found the half-full bag of crushed cans behind the kitchen bin. He took them outside to the yard and poured them into the recycle bin.

    At least I have something to talk about with drill holes when I'm next in the dole shop, he thought. On his way back inside the house, Spruyt slapped the top of the dusty steel BBQ.

  The tiny landing was littered with dust-coloured boxes. In a fit of productivity, he'd started clearing out his room. Boxes and boxes of memories hoarded for the mere purpose of building a wall between himself and the present. A fort of lame escapism. It all had to go. This room had started as the spare room, and now Spruyt was determined to get it back to that.

  Eight or so boxes deep, Spruyt picked up a tattered piece of pink cloth from inside a long-forgotten box. Freeing it from the box completely, a thinner pink fizz burst out. He let it unfold to reveal the tutu, Marie's one relic of happiness with her parents. Holding each shoulder strap, he held it high and in front of him for a full inspection. Spruyt felt a pain in his heart as he saw the rips from his shoulders and barrel chest from when he forced it on. After some time, he'd decided what he had to do. He folded it back up, as careful as a monk rolling up a sacred parchment and placed it to one side.

Marie got the car after everything went wonky between them, so he called Thom. Between them, it took over two hours to get all the unwanted stuff into the car, down to the skip, dealt with and back again. In that entire time, they spoke about everything but work. Spruyt got the impression Thom had somehow got wind of the hospital visit based on certain things he said and how he acted with him. Asking Spruyt if he should be doing any heavy lifting, how have you been resting etc. He responded with the most non-committal answers whilst remaining chippy, receptive. He didn't mind the company, in fact, it was nice, but it couldn't go into the detailed stuff. Not yet, anyway.

    When Thom dropped him off for the final time, Spruyt retrieved the toolbox from the cupboard under the sink and climbed the narrow stairs. He began to take the bed and wardrobe apart. It was time to move into the present.

The suit looked like a hung man. Its musty smell filled the room making Spruyt feel damp himself. He stood looking at it, feeling the nerves bounce around his stomach like a pinball. Thom had phoned again about the job; the meeting was now set in stone. There was no foreplay, no working into it, he just came right out and put in a date and time. It had to happen, Spruyt knew this, but it didn't subside his fear any. Was society ready to welcome him back? Was he ready for society again? There was too much he didn't know. It dawned on him, eventually, that it'd always be this way. So either defecate or get off the pot, he thought.

Spruyt came back with the sellotape, the suit was covered in lint. He tore a strip from the roll and began to pat the suit down.

The knock at the door was aggressive. Spruyt ran to answer it, it sounded urgent. On opening it, he saw a child. Well, he was about eighteen or nineteen, face pitted in acne scars and a mean look in his eyes. Wearing a high-vis waistcoat and a black baseball cap, he had a parcel in his hands along with a clipboard. The kid looked intently at Spruyt for a moment after the door had been opened. He then broke his gaze and looked down at his clipboard.

'Mr...Spry?'

'Why not,' Spruyt replied. That's a new one, he thought. He made a mental note to add that to the list of words people had guessed when trying to say his name.

'Sign here, please.'

He did just that. The kid handed over the parcel and turned to leave. Spruyt didn't even wait to get back inside. He ripped it open on his doorstep. Holding it high for a full inspection, he smiled. In front of the kid and the whole partially-vacated street, Spruyt stood holding the pink garment in all its repaired glory. 'It's perfect,' he said to no one.

He saw Beth again too. Spruyt was shaking while he waited for her. He'd arrived early and was led to his table like a cow, calmly walked across the room by the waiter. He ordered a coke and sat down. The ice-cold glass arrived and before the waiter had even turned he'd downed it and asked for another. Perplexed, the waiter took the empty away.

He was convinced it wouldn't be how it was. The flow won't be there, the connection. It was all fleeting. He inspected his thumb that he cut some time ago; barely a cut there now. Just the scab the size of a raspberry seed. Spruyt put this thumb in his mouth and began to bite down on the nail. The cycles of criticism and self-doubt continued to whirl around his head while he chomped on his own flesh.

The waiter returned with his fresh drink. Beth soon followed, which caused him to rip his thumb out of his face. He caught his front teeth as he did this, which made a dull snapping sound like a bone breaking. As she waved and said hello, Spruyt burped in reply.

'They told me you could charm the chastity belt off of queen Victoria.'

'Actions are more powerful than nukes,' he said. He'd never hated himself so much, which given his recent past was quite a feat, but to say something like that whilst letting himself get caught sucking his thumb and burping...

He was a child.

Afterbirth

There's a clearness in his eyes, Beth thought, a shine. She'd watched him only drink water or coke as they spoke. He must be off the schooners, she pondered, and she felt a wave of pride wash over her. A need to hug him too. It was almost maternal the feeling she got from seeing how he held himself, his patter and gestures. There was a freedom to them, all which he didn't have way back when. She'd decided to leave her hair down this time and this was playing on her mind. She was self-conscious about her neck, so she would often use her long mane to smother it. The night she first bumped into Spruyt, she was experimenting in styles. A swing and a miss, she'd decided. Still, she brushes the right-hand side of her strands behind her ear. This exposed her fault and she felt fine about it. She hadn't felt this way around someone in time. To be so comfortable with a person. This oddball was fine by her.

Spruyt wanted to down his second glass of coke. It was a reflex from his old vice, of course, but the muscle memory of his arm and mouth was telling him he'd feel better if he did it. He fought the urge for most of the meal. Beth too looked different. He wasn't sure how, but she looked better than the first time. Her lithe body and engaging facial expressions pulled him in. She wasn't just there out of pity or morbid interest or to escape from her own life, she was just *there*. In the moment. taking in him, the malbec she drank, the meat paella she ate, the feel of the table cloth or the chair under her. It was all being appreciated, enjoyed.

    I could sit there for hours just watching her, Spruyt thought.

It was harder than he planned, trying to get Marie's new address. He couldn't bring himself to speak to her parents or her closest friends. Through his cracked phone, he tried to get her address from her socials. Marie wasn't daft though, to leave her full address on the big scary world-wide-web. How dare she be so sensible, Spruyt thought. He was left with no other option; he reached out to Austin's. They had a contact address but could not give it out. It took some time, but they managed to come to an agreement.

Afterbirth

A few days later, he walked to their office, which took over an hour. The sun was present but not warm. The air was still, the traffic around him sparse. His lungs felt good. On arriving, he dropped the parcel off. Austin's were to call Marie the next day and advise she had a parcel waiting for her. It's not much, Spruyt knew, but hopefully, it would help her.

'Spruyt,' the burly voice called. It shook him out of his mindless slumber, with the weeks of caffeine withdrawal sitting on his shoulders. The wooden chair creaked under his weight, the padding long worn down by generations of arses that had used it. With his head whizzing around on his swan-like neck, he tried to find the source of his summons. A somewhat heavyset woman, in her forties onwards, stood with her arms folded on her chest. Her hair was pulled back aggressively in a slick bun, exposing a very shiny forehead. Clutching at her massive jugs & a notepad covered in hieroglyphs someone sarcastically called English, Spruyt remembered she was the one waiting for him. The voice was far too husky for her but he'd made that mistake before. Chuckling to himself at that distant memory, Spruyt stood up and followed her.

Shiny head led him to a booth made of a desk, an empty chair for the evaluator & one semi-clear screen to split the large desk from one into two. Spruyt could hear the laughing of two elderly women coming from the otherside of the partition. Scratching and looking at his elbow, he swallowed hard and said, 'Thank you.'

'For?'

'You got my name right,' Spruyt released his elbow and met her gaze, 'It can be frustrating to be mislabelled all the time, you know?'

Shiny head smiled and then looked at her clipboard. Spruyt had never seen her smile before. In fact, apart from his evaluator with his fake smile, he'd never seen anyone here smile genuinely. Seekers or staffers, never. It felt nice to cause a positive emotion for a change.

She said through that rare smile, 'You take care now, Mr Spruyt.'

Afterbirth

He sat up for a change. With his back ruler-straight and both legs planted firmly on the floor instead of being crossed or twitching, he took a deep inhale of breath. He felt calm, there was no creeping embarrassment or anger or fear. I wish I had a book with me, Spruyt thought. That was a new thought for him and it was one he decided to follow through with on his way home. Smiling to himself, when the evaluator took his seat, he mistook Spruyt's gaze for a greeting.

'Mr..?' And with that, normal service was resumed. The English are so arrogant when it comes to language, anything outside the box and they flounder. Panic in the waters of pronunciation. Spruyt was still smiling as the evaluator fumbled around his words. Judging by his top-button-done-straight-as-an-arrow-tie-soaked-in-old-spice demeanour, and all the recent history Spruyt could remember, there was about a zero-to-one odd he'd get it right.

'Mr...Mr Sprout?'

'Nope,' he was still smiling as he said this.

™© *Z M Barrett*

'Oh dear, is it Sprunt?'

'Close, but no kaleidoscope.'

'Go on then sir, enlighten me please.'

'Why not,' he mumbled. Spruyt told him how it was supposed to be said, as far as he knew.

'Excellent, excellent...' His neck hung loose with flesh, shagging but somehow wrinkle-free. Eyes buried so deep they looked like drill holes. Spruyt brought each of his hands up to hold the opposite shoulder. It was immature body language from a supposed adult. A diet adult, maybe. Spruyt heard another explosion of horrible hyena laughter from the otherside of the partition. He joined his companion by staring across at the blurred wall of the next space. Still looking there & smiling, Spruyt heard him say,

'So, how are we today Mr Spruyt?'

Sniffing up hard through his nose brought a clear gust of air and nothing more. Dropping his hands from his shoulders, he took a moment to compose himself before answering. I wonder if he'll hear me or just brush past it like normal, Spruyt pondered. He

Afterbirth

dropped his head down momentarily before replying.

Spruyt said, 'Well, I've been on a journey of some self-discovery, recently. I now realise that the past is a prison. If you want day release or permanent freedom you have to work at it, by yourself, rehabilitate, so you can be trusted with your present and future, you know?'

'Excellent, excellent,' bringing his focus from the partition to the paper in front of him, his fake smile was wiped off. It didn't fade, it was just gone. It's business time. 'So, you've been on the allowance for…eleven months or so?' Spruyt didn't know or care and wanted to say as such, but couldn't. Answers were not only being listened to but noted for good measure. He answered in the affirmative, through a mumble or nod or both.

'Righto. Now, since your last visit, what have you done to find gainful employment since your last signing on date?' Spruyt wound up his smile again. Setting his face in the most happy-go-lucky look he could muster, he replied,

'Nothing.'

™© *Z M Barrett*

The evaluator actually ripped his gaze from his precious paperwork. Shock widened his eyes before he replied, 'Come again?'

'I've done nothing. Zip. Nil, bupkis.'

'So, we've had *no* progress then?' Such a preposterous statement, Spruyt thought. First off, progress is a relative term. The past weeks had seen vast progress in the following; learning to cook vegetable & fish inspired dishes (pan-fried mackerel, chillies and rice was his new favourite), dropping his coffee intake to one cup a week (the rest replaced with herbal tea, it's horrible) and had taken all his alcohol intake to zero. His body felt better, his cramps had lessened in severity and occurrence. In Spruyt's eyes, this was progress. Something gained, something learned. He briefly pondered whether drill holes would like to hear about the throwing out of the crushed cans but decided against it.

But, thinking all that, he also knew this would not be progress for tiny eyes here. And secondly, we? Come on guy, at what point are *you* involved? Spruyt was biting through his lip at this point trying not to say this, trying not to say anything to drill holes that you are not even involved in these visits. Asking banal questions and then handing me a ticket to move on, an Argos of unwanted labour, useless members of this here great society. Spruyt wanted to say all this, turned all this around in his thoughts, but what he actually said was, 'Correct. I have an interview later this week, for my old job, but this is more out of pity than anything else, you understand. Who knows how it will play out.' He let out a small, laboured cough.

Drill holes held his gaze with Spruyt. He wasn't smiling but he also wasn't writing. 'Listen,' Spruyt continued, 'I'm just being honest with you.'

'Sir, you do realise we can cut you off if you haven't been keeping up your side of the signed agreement to seek part or full-time employment?'

'Does the pope harvest people's prayers for his own ego?'

'Come again?'

'The answer is yes, he does.' Spruyt wondered if drill holes was a religious man or not. This could push some reactionary buttons. Spruyt saw him pout former leader-of-the-free world style in thought. He had no idea what he would say next.

'How cynical, Mr Spruyt. I see him more as an encourage-er of connection with the universe and the world around us.'

Spruyt pondered on this. Perhaps, he thought. Then he said,

'Well, are you religious?'

'No sir, I am not. This doesn't mean I can't appreciate other people's beliefs.'

'How cultured. I doth my cap to you, sire.' Spruyt thought for abit more before adding, 'I'd say I'm more spiritually deaf than anything. I can't hear the good or the bad of religion.' Drill holes felt like he was lost in a heavy mist at sea. What is this young man on about, he pondered.

Spruyt had never understood religion, it always seemed like a cop-out to him. A lazy move. The sin is not in the killing of a god, Spruyt thought, but the creating of one.

'But we digress; tell me more about this interview?' So, Spruyt told him. He downplayed it as a sympathy date-type thing, something that will most likely end in nothing but an experience, a going through the motions type deal, a non-event. Again, nervously for Spruyt, drill holes held his gaze.

Cue a very restrained, 'excellent, excellent…' It was only then he noticed that his neck rippled like fleshy water when he spoke.

Drill holes looked back down to his paper and started to note something. The scribble of a pen against paper filled Spruyt's ears until it was broken by the rip of a ticket.

'So, here is your number Mr Spruyt. If you'd check the automated job kiosks on your way out if you haven't already, it would be very much appreciated. You have a great day now.' He offered the ticket out to Spruyt, who stood up and leaned over to take it. Grasping the ticket, he held it there for a moment or two. Still holding his eye contact with those dark spots that should have eyes, he tried to gauge what drill holes was thinking. All he could see was the shadows of his eye sockets and his fat neck. Spruyt wanted to take all this in, as for some unholy reason, he knew whatever happened, he wouldn't be back here again.

'You too, amigo.'

™© *Z M Barrett*

It was time. Spruyt had been pottering around his house for hours. Waiting until the last minute to put his suit on. Bennigan's wasn't far from his house, which meant travel wasn't an issue. With the meeting being early afternoon, the middle of the day, it left Spruyt stuck. He couldn't start anything but at the same time, it was a long wait. He had to put the suit on at some point, but why put it on and sit around the house not feeling comfortable? But then again, just waiting around in your shorts and tee's made you too comfortable when you should really be focused on what is to come. Spruyt was in a real no-man's land of how to spend his free time that day. There was a lot of pacing, self-inspired pep-talks, cycles of doubt and drinks of water. It didn't kill the time, it just prolonged it. Eventually, Spruyt made the call to get ready.

    Walking into his new room, the main bedroom, the suit hung over him like a shadow. It'd been some time that he'd been living in that room and he still wasn't used to it. Having so much space, much more light

Afterbirth

from the east-facing window, not being surrounded by the boxes and the past they contained. It was scary for him still, to be this new guy. It was a good scary, though. He turned towards his hanging tormentor, the dark material of smartness and promise and professionalism.

It looked like a hungman from the gallows whilst it was waiting on its hanger and once he put it on, Spruyt felt the same. Adjusting his tie (it took him eight attempts just to get the knot right) he felt wide. Heavy in the gut and hips. Still, black was thinning, right? Spruyt pondered on this for a moment. He decided he looked more like a black hole than a professional.

After descending the narrow stairs, he still had some time to kill, a few minutes before he had to leave. Entering the kitchen, he battled with himself about making a brew or not. He decided, eventually, against it. This said, he'd still got the 'UNT' cup off the side and put the teabag in it. The kettle had even been switched on before he shouted no at himself and clicked it off again. Spruyt leaned back against the countertop and folded his arms. His right hand brushed against something small on the inside pocket of his jacket. A lighter, maybe, or a pen. He didn't smoke or write, so he decided to investigate it. Reaching inside the pocket, he pulled out a pack of very dated chewing gum. The logo would have been the height of trend and culture for the ninety eighties, he thought. With nothing else better to do, he took out a piece and began to chew on it. It was horrible, dated. It tasted like head and shoulders.

    Mercifully, the time came. Spruyt left the house.

The place hadn't changed at all, Spruyt thought. It was still the same generic building, built in the seventies and no longer fit for modern purpose. Bricks crumbling away into sand, wooden window frames cracked and splintering all the past layers of paint that had been used floating in the air like snowflakes, blinds older than him dancing in the light breeze from the second floor onwards where windows had been cracked open. The glass of the windows and doors had that binge tint to it, like it had been dyed by the decades of sunlight. The colour always reminded Spruyt of his auntie, whenever he visited her she would make him a brew in a clear mug made of the same coloured glass.

Standing there, Spruyt wished someone could come out and get him. No, there has been too much of that, he spat at himself. He approached the door like a cat, careful little paw steps, trying not to spook the building or himself. Grabbing the handle, Spruyt tried the door. It didn't open, it just rattled in its frame. He tried a second and third time with the same result. Looking up from the handle, he saw the main reception for the building. A lady, around his age, with a kings of leon blue-grass bangs haircut and specs the size of satellite dishes, stood up behind the counter. Spruyt knew his constant rattling of the door had raised her from the seat. She was smiling politely whilst pointing downwards. Spruyt followed her action and saw a speaker grill with a few buttons on it. The handwritten signs stuck under each button had long rubbed away. He lent down and said, 'Sorry.'

Nothing happened. Spruyt repeated the same action and got nothing in return. He looked back through the dim glass to the lady. Still smiling, she shook her head in the negative, then cupped one of her hands to her hidden ear. When she stopped shaking her head, she motioned with her free hand at pushing something. It took Spruyt another few moments before he realised she meant he had to push one of the buttons to talk to her. Mercifully, he guessed the right button on his first asking.

Holding the button in and looking back at the speaker grill, Spruyt said, 'Sorry.' Releasing the button, another crackle of static greeted him before a thin robot voice spoke back.

'It's okay dear, we never had to do this. You can't have open doors these days, you never know who could walk in!'

'Very true,' Spruyt responded. Waiting, he looked back up from the speaker to the lady inside the building. Both waited for the other one to talk. Eventually, another crackled walkie-talkie voice said, 'Can I help you, dear?'

'Oh right, it would help if I explained wouldn't it?' He laughed at his awkwardness, still holding the button in, he spoke to the lady and not the grill, explaining why he was here. A loud alarm buzz sounded off, and this time the door let Spruyt in.

He was now sitting in the reception for Bennigan's. With a magazine open in his lap, he stared ahead. The plastic smell of the fresh pages loitered in his nose. On this floor, the old decore had been ripped out and replaced with the steel clear greys of modern minimalism. There were no walls, just a clear glass of separation. It was young glass too, not like the binge-tinted glass of outside, this was clear as fresh crystal. Thom was behind one of these faux walls, headset on and sealing deals, probably. With both hands free, he spoke in a very animated way, yet you could hear nothing but the gentle hum of the A/C.

    The girl had no reception bank to hide behind, it was just a tiny desk with a tablet stand and one of those chairs that folded your legs back-underneath you for the best sitting posture. Spruyt couldn't take in what she looked like or what she was doing, though, he'd wandered away in his head again. A little grumble from his gut had got him looking for a hayfield again. He let out a small, laboured cough. The magazine slipped through the gap in his legs onto the floor. The stale piece of gum was still in his mouth but Spruyt had forgotten to chew on it since he'd entered the building. His mouth was dry, the palms of his hands soaked. Someone's voice went off in front of him, but it sounded distant and muffled. Like it had been underwater.

'Sorry?'

'Thom, he's running late for your meeting. He won't be long now, Mr...' Spruyt bent down and retrieved the magazine he hadn't realised he'd dropped. Be nice, he thought, don't let the poor girl stuffer.

'It's Paul, and thanks.'

She laughed and thanked him. He now noticed a pleading in her eyes, she wanted to know how his name was said. I'll save that, he thought. That way, if this thing goes completely tits up, at least she'll still remember me. He could see it now, in his mind's-eye, her talking to Thom or Sue or whoever, saying something like, 'and what about that guy with the mad name, whatever happened to him?' Spruyt joined in with her laughter before they both stopped. He felt warm, internally. An emotional warmth which settled his nerves and gut.

'Ahh, here he is, the biggest "UNT" I know!' Thom had burst through his clear door as he said this. More laughter erupted from the girl as Spruyt smiled with a wry chuckle too. Standing up, he said, 'I deserved that.'

Joining Thom, Spruyt felt his arm land on his shoulders. He was prattling on about something, some deal he'd just closed or such, but Spruyt wasn't listening. Walking through the office door with Thom, he realised this was more than just walking into a meeting, an interview, whatever. He felt, with utter conviction, that this was it. All that pain and nonsense of his former life was now in its right linear place. He thought about Beth, about Marie, about Thom and all the new memories they would share together. Spruyt turned and closed the clear door to the office. He closed over his past to let it dissolve peacefully. He was no longer stumbling through the fog, he was now in the clear. The smile he was holding on his face made him feel light-headed, accepted, relevant and needed. When the door clicked shut, he fought back the urge to let out a laboured cough. There was no need for that now.

About the author

ZMB was born in North Wales and grew up in idyllic villages of the summer and the aggressive winter surf of the coastline. He moved to study music in Liverpool before adopting the city as his home. When he isn't writing or reading or annoying his few friends and patient family, he still picks up the acoustic and drum sticks. Occasionally the bass too, although his bass-face isn't what it once was.

Someday, he will reach his dream of becoming one of the infamous buskers of Bold street.

Someday.

™© *Z M Barrett*

Printed in Great Britain
by Amazon